When A Savage Falls For A Good Girl:

A Crazy Hood Love

Tina J

Copyright 2020

When I'm alone in my room, sometimes I stare at the wall, automatic weapons on the floor but who can you call, my down bitch, one who live by the code. Ashton Martin by Rick Ross played on my beats pill as I prepared myself for tonight. I hated when niggas couldn't do their jobs and I had to step in. What the fuck am I paying them for?

I stood in the mirror fixing my clothes, with a blunt hanging out the side of my mouth. The bullet proof vest fit snug, and the small Glock 26 was wrapped around my ankle. If ever I ran outta bullets, this one always came in handy. The two regular Glocks were in holsters on my waist. The hunter's knife was in a sheath holder I found on amazon. Whenever I went to battle as I call it, I made sure to be fully equipped and ready for anything.

I backed away from the mirror, locked the bedroom door, went to my closet and pressed a button. The walls went in, to the side and brought up all the shelves filled with different weapons. No one knows about this; not even my girl.

When I say, I trusted no one but my boy, Jamaica; I trusted no one. We call him that because it's where he came from. His real name is Kenron but ain't no one calling him that.

I have two brothers and I look at them sideways because they sheisty as hell. They can't be trusted either. One is two years older than me and the other one is ten. The youngest one stay robbing family members and my mom laughs it off. I told that nigga I'd chop his fucking hands off if he ever stole from me. He ain't been to my house since. Yup, he can get it too.

My older brother is the pretty boy type. Not that I'm ugly because that's not the case. I'm brown skinned, almost chocolate. I kept my hair in a ceaser haircut and my goatee is low as well. I'm not with that beard shit because when my girl wants her pussy ate, I don't want cum inside. Some men like it but not me.

People ask if my brother and I are twins all the time because we look so much alike. We definitely resemble but not ~~we're~~ *where* people should mistake us for twins. Then again, I can't tell you what they see.

5

Anyway, he travels a lot with his insurance job to different states and sometimes countries. I asked what kind of insurance he selling because ain't no job sending you overseas unless you're the owner, and that, he's not. He tells me to mind my business and it's exactly what I do. If he gets caught up in some shit, I'ma still be minding my business. His ass can go to jail for all I care. I bet he won't last a day with his conceited ass. Nigga can't fight either. They'll have a ball with him in there. If shit gets too bad then of course, I'll help but until it happens, he does him and I do me.

Standing in the closet, I smiled at all my toys. There were revolvers, shotguns, semi-automatic, pistols and assault rifles. Another wall, held full metal bullets, hollow point, LRN, FMJ and a whole lot more. On the far left, the wall held different knives, machetes, chains and anything else you can imagine. You name a weapon and nine times out of ten, it's in my closet.

"Baby, why is the door locked?" I heard my girl Zahra ask on the other side. I grabbed the bag holding the semi-automatic I needed, checked for bullets, pressed the button for the walls to close and hurried to put my shirt on. I opened the door slowly and stared at how sexy she looked.

Zahra isn't your average chicken head and took pride in herself. Her appearance has never been off, even on a bad day. She lived on the other side of town in a condo and drove a brand-new Maserati truck, I purchased for her. She had her own money but I never had an issue spoiling her because she deserved it.

We've been together for four years and I've never fucked another woman. Not gonna say bitches didn't suck me off but no one can ever claim to bed me. Yea, most consider it cheating but hey, if my girl don't like giving head I gotta get it from somewhere. I'm not gonna say she's opposed to doing it but she can't suck dick for shit. When she does try, I get pissed off so to avoid it, I don't even ask. I tried to coach her but it's always, *I don't like it or what if you cum in my mouth?* Who wants to hear that shit?

Zahra is aware and never says anything because it's not like I get it done and run home to tell her. She may be ok with it, but there's no need to throw it in her face. The few bitches who I do get head from, know not to approach her or open their mouths. Let's just say, I'm known to be a straight savage and any and every knows it. Therefore; they make sure to keep me happy.

"I didn't realize it was locked."

"Even if I were away, why is it locked?" She peeked around me I guess to see if any other women were in here.

"Ain't nobody here."

"Better not be." I pulled her close and pecked her lips.

"What you doing here anyway? I thought you'd be gone for a few more days." She's a traveling nurse and visits different hospitals to assist doctors. I asked why she didn't get a job at the hospital. She claims traveling pays better. I don't really care because she's working and it gives us space so we're not up under each other all the time.

"You don't miss me?" Her arms went around my neck.

"I always miss you." I placed a kiss on her neck and felt her hands going to my buckle.

"Not right now Zahra." I moved her out the way and headed down stairs. I hated to leave knowing we haven't had sex since she left almost a week ago. Unfortunately, I had shit to do but I did promise to tear her pussy up when I came back.

"Kruz, I've began gone for six days. The least you can do is fuck me before you go do whatever." I stopped in my tracks and turned to look at her.

"What I tell you about that shit?" I dropped the bag and walked back up the steps.

"I'm sorry Kruz." She attempted to go in the room but I caught her. My hand slid in her long mane, gripped it tight and forced her to look at me. I could sense the fear and it wasn't my intention but she knew I hated her to throw tantrums. If you're a grown woman, then act like one. She knows damn well I'll give her what she wants but right now I can't.

"Don't bring your ass to my motherfucking crib popping shit about me fucking you." She nodded her head.

"You talking like these bitches on the street and you're better than that."

"I'm sorry. I miss you and..."

"I miss you too but when I have shit to do, my girl is supposed to have my back. She's not supposed to nag me when I'm tryna stay focused."

"Ok." She said above a whisper.

"I can't hear you." I moved my ear closer to her mouth.

"I won't bother you before work again." I released her hair and stared in her eyes. Something was off. I'm not sure what it was but I felt it.

"What's wrong?" I moved away, crossed my arms and stared at her.

"Where the fuck you been over the last few days?"

"What?" The nervous look plagued her face. *BINGO!*

"Where were you?"

"Working Kruz. You know that."

"Hmph." I continued staring and once the fidgeting began I knew something was up. She lost eye contact with me and I could see how uncomfortable I made her.

In four years, my girl has never been weak, scary or insecure; until today. Then again, she's never come home

10

telling me I better fuck her after being gone either. She's usually understanding and has no problem waiting for me to return.

"STRIP!" I barked and Zahra jumped.

"Excuse me."

"You heard what the fuck I said. Take all your fucking clothes off."

"Kruz?"

"NOW!" One thing people knew about me is when I got angry, the best thing to do is comply with my demand.

Zahra began removing them slowly. Each second passing, I sensed how terrified she was. The only thing is, she wasn't terrified of me. She was terrified of what I may see. Afraid of whatever secret she's hiding; accidently coming to light. Call me paranoid all you want but I'm no fool. I can spot a bullshitter, manipulator, con-artist and pretender anywhere. I felt my phone vibrating on my hip and kept my gaze on her. Whoever it is, can wait.

"Turn around."

"Is this necessary?" She did like I asked. One would think I'd be turned on but I'm far from being horny.

"I pushed her against the wall, stuck two fingers inside her pussy, pulled them out and sniffed."

"GET THE FUCK OUT MY HOUSE!" I wiped her juices on the clothes I just tossed in her face.

"What?"

"NOW! GET THE FUCK OUT!" I grabbed her arm and drug her down the steps.

"Kruz, you're bugging." I let go and stared at her.

"I'm bugging huh?" She started putting her clothes on. I stopped her before she could put her panties on.

"Let me show you why I'm bugging as you say." I grabbed my phone and noticed the missed call from Jamaica. I'll call him back.

"Lay on the couch."

"What for?"

"JUST DO IT!" She was so scared she fell over the side and landed with her legs cocked open.

"Stay just like that." I pressed the flashlight on my phone, put it to her pussy and spread her legs a little wider. I used my finger to dig for what I felt earlier and pulled it out.

"This is why the fuck you need to get out." I showed her the rim of the condom and she covered her mouth.

When I stuck my fingers in between her legs I felt something weird. I knew it wasn't skin and automatically assumed it to be a rubber. She must've fucked some nigga and the condom broke off.

"Kruz, let me explain." I chuckled at her ignorance.

"Explain what? How you came in my crib popping shit about fucking you and some nigga already been in it. Bitch, I would've fucked you with another nigga's condom and possible sperm in you. You a nasty ass bitch. Get the fuck out." I tried to remain calm but every second I thought about it pissed me off more.

"We've been together for, four years Zahra and not once did we ever use a condom. Therefore; you really don't have shit to say to me." She started crying and usually her tears would get to me but not this time. I sat on the loveseat and pulled the small nine out my sock.

"The way I see it is, you cheated and I don't even care how many times."

"Kruz, you allowed bitches to suck you off." I knew one day she'd try an throw it in my face.

"BECAUSE YOU FUCKING TOLD ME TOO." I shouted.

"Your exact words were, *Kruz baby, I'll do it for you but it's not something I like doing. If you want this done, I give you permission but you can't fuck no other bitches. I won't accuse you of cheating because I'm allowing it.*"

"I didn't mean for you to go out and really do it."

"Then you shouldn't have said it." I told her through gritted teeth.

"I was ok with you not doing it. You're the one who pushed me into it." She put her head down because she knew I was right.

"You have fifteen; no seven seconds to bounce or I promise to lay you the fuck out."

14

"Baby, we can get through this."

"Five seconds." I put one bullet in my gun. I'm about to play Russian roulette with her ass and she better hope she survives.

"Kruz?" I pointed my gun at her.

CLICK! She jumped.

"Oh my God!"

CLICK! I watched her run out the front door half naked.

"Oh shit yo!" Jamaica laughed on the way in.

"I love you Kruz. Please stop this." She stood at the truck door crying.

CLICK! I could tell she was getting more nervous.

"Watch this." I pulled my gun off my waist, placed a silencer on it, aimed it at the truck pulling off and watched the back-windshield shatter. I aimed at the tires and each one blew. She tried to steer the truck but it was no use. It slammed into the front gate. I walked over with Jamaica behind me.

"You ain't leaving with shit I brought you. Tell that nigga to buy you one." I yanked her out the truck, had my boy back it up and tossed her on the ground. If you even think about coming through these gates again, you will fucking regret it. Play with me if you want." I pressed the button for them to close.

"I'm sorry Kruz. It was a mistake. Please don't do this. I'm pregnant." I stopped and ran my hand over my face.

"Stay in contact with my mother. When the child is born, I'll have a DNA test done. If the child is mine, we'll co-parent and that's it. You are officially dead to me." I spoke without turning around. She didn't deserve to see my face.

"KRUZZZZZZ!" She screamed out. I wiped the few tears running down my face, walked in my house and slammed the door.

"You good bro?" Jamaica handed me a shot.

"I've never in my life cried over a bitch."

"Shit happens. You wanna cancel the hit for tonight?"

"Yea. My mind ain't right and you know how I feel about going somewhere unfocused." He nodded, turned the television on in the living room and copped a squat on the couch. I'll see him in the morning because I'm sure he's staying the night.

I went upstairs, took everything off and started bagging all her shit up. She may have her own place but she had a closet full of stuff here. Clothes, shoes, purses, coats and anything her heart desired. There's nothing I wouldn't have done for her and now she's claiming to be pregnant. It only makes leaving her alone difficult.

My mother is gonna want me to be a father and that's not a problem but she's the old-fashioned type to want us to live together. She's very big on family and Zahra is the perfect woman for me in her eyes. I already know once she finds out, my phone will ring off the hook.

After packing her stuff up and throwing it in the trash cans outside, I took my ass to bed. I needed to be focused to handle my shit tomorrow.

"Can you come pick me up please?" I cried in the phone to my sister, Kalila. I didn't wanna call her but I had no friends. She's the only one I knew would come.

"Where are you and why does it sound like you're crying?" I sucked my teeth because once I mentioned what went down, I can hear her talking shit.

When I originally started cheating on Kruz, it was supposed to be a one-time thing. It escalated and the two of us met frequently when I went to work. My sister only found out because she was using my phone one day and he sent an explicit text message. Her nosy ass opened it and read it.

Long story short, she told me to stop cheating or leave Kruz alone. My greedy ass continued doing both and now look. I'm standing out here in just a shirt and bra, with no panties, jeans or even shoes on.

"Kruz broke up with me." I wiped the tears and snot falling down my face.

"Ok, so drive your ass home."

"He took the truck." I whispered.

18

"I can't hear you Zahra."

"HE TOOK THE TRUCK DAMMIT. HE FOUND OUT I CHEATED AND SHOT THE WINDOWS OUT." She busted out laughing.

"I told your stupid ass to stop cheating on him." She hung up. I dialed her back.

"WHAT?" She snapped.

"Are you coming?" She blew her breath in the phone.

"Yea. Let me drop Rhythm off and I'll be right there." I rolled my eyes. I hated her best friend. They've been friends since elementary school and secretly I despised their relationship. You would swear they were sisters more than the two of us were.

"Hurry up please."

"Bitch, don't rush me because yo ho ass got caught." She hung up laughing. I had no one to blame but myself for the situation I'm in. It's not like I planned on cheating. It just happened a year ago.

"Damn, you sexy." He said and instead of ignoring him like I should've, I entertained it.

19

Kruz and I had an argument over me moving in with him. We had been together for three years at this time and I felt we should live together. He has always said; a woman won't reside with him permanently unless she's his wife. I could respect that but he's spoken about me being his wife and even asked what type of ring I wanted. So what's the problem with us living together? I stormed out the house and ended up at the local bar.

"What you want?"

"You." He said it with ease. I stared at him and smiled. I don't know why he came at me but this man is forbidden fruit and I knew it. Instead of telling him to beat it, we stayed at the bar drinking and laughing until closing.

"Let's take this over to my place."

"Yea right." I laughed it off. He lifted me over his shoulder, walked me out the bar and straight to his car. Being intoxicated, I let my body betray me and went with the flow.

The minute we got to his house, he wasted no time taking my clothes off. Thank goodness it was late and he stayed in a different area because he damn sure had my ass moaning in the driveway. Yup, we fucked outside with no care in the world. It was reckless as fuck and so was allowing him to cum in me all night.

"I knew your pussy would be good." He whispered in my ear. I realized it was the next day and jumped up.

"Don't worry. Your car is out front and my lips are sealed if you have a man." He licked is lips and for some reason my pussy began throbbing. Needless to say, we fucked again and been together ever since.

I don't know why I cheated when nothing was lacking at home with Kruz. The sex was out of this world, he gave me whatever I wanted and the amount of street power he had, had me feeling like a queen. People I didn't even know gave me respect.

If a bitch tried popping shit, someone would shut it down fast, or one of the hood rats Kruz knew, would beat their ass for me. He never wanted me acting ratchet or ghetto. He said, his queen had to remain perfect and never lower her standards to peasants. His famous line was always, *"Those bitches don't got shit to lose so they don't mind being ignorant.*" I should've listened. I blame my pussy though. No one told her to be attracted to another man and give herself to him.

BEEEEEEEEP! I heard and looked up to see my sister and her dirty ass friend in the front seat.

"I thought you were dropping her off. Now she gonna be all in my business."

"Girl, don't nobody care what you going through." Rhythm waved me off and stayed in the front seat.

"Damn, this is nice." My sister said looking at the house.

In the four years Kruz and I were together, I never brought her here. He's only met her and my mom a few times and that's because he picked me up from there. Say what you want, but I was selfish when it came to Kruz. If I could keep him away from the world, I would.

"Move." I still had the front door opened, staring at Rhythm.

"Ugh, get your ass in the back." She smirked when my sister said it.

"I am not riding in the back so this bitch could ride in the front."

"Bitch?" She questioned and stepped out.

"Either get yo ass in the back or stay the fuck out here. I don't really give a fuck." If you're wondering, me and my sister don't see eye to eye either. I blame this Rhythm bitch. Had she let me and my sister bond growing up this wouldn't be going on. I slammed the door and pouted moving in the back seat.

"Cover your pussy. My son don't need to see that." Her son was in the back asleep. She threw her jacket in the back and if he wasn't here, I'd smack the fuck outta her from the back. It wouldn't be the first fight we had.

A few years ago, her baby daddy tried to talk to me. This was before I met Kruz and still in college. She had just birthed their son and he wasn't tryna wait for sex. His words, not mine. I wasn't trying to give him the time of day but she assumed otherwise. I guess when she caught him grabbing my ass, it was game on. She swung and we fought. I can admit she gave me a run for my money until he separated us.

Come to find out, he had already been stepping out and she thought I was the chick. Little did she know, I fucked him way before she did. I never mentioned it because he was strictly for money purposes only. His dick game is good but he had too much going on.

I wanted a man who only had eyes for me. A man to give me whatever I asked for and didn't care how much something costs. A man who appreciated a woman going to school to better herself and one who didn't have a bunch of bitches on the side. That's when Kruz came along and showed me what it's like to be loved. I mean, really loved. You know that fairytale love that makes you wanna sit up under him all day and night.

Kruz was the perfect gentleman when we met and his looks were exotic. He was Dominican with beautiful hair that he eventually cut off. His body was built like a professional boxer and tattoos lined his body.

One in particular stood out and it was a heart on his chest with an empty box in the middle. I asked why was it empty and he told me, the woman's name he married will go in there. I wanted that name to be mine so every bitch would know he belonged to me. Unfortunately, I doubt it will be me but at least we'll still be together because of our child. Yes, the child is his. The other guy and I only slipped up once and I took a plan b. We were extra careful up until last night.

See, he's been meeting me when I go out of town. This morning we had sex before separating and he mentioned the condom breaking. However, I had no idea remnants of it were still in my pussy. The look on Kruz face will haunt me forever. I knew he loved me and even though I allowed him to let women suck his dick, I knew he never slept with them. I shouldn't have let him but I didn't wanna do it. No specific reason on why and he told me plenty of times he refused to let a woman do what I should but I pushed him to it. Actually, I watched it go down the first time in the strip club.

Kruz was fucked up and I excused myself to use the bathroom. I found one of the strippers coming out the room and asked if she wanted to make extra money. She told me yes and asked what she had to do. When I mentioned Kruz's name, she hopped on it. Low and behold, she went in VIP, danced for him and sucked him off.

The next day I told him what happened and he apologized over and over for slipping. I told him it was ok and he stopped speaking to me for days. He claims, I shouldn't be ok with it but after telling him I'll never be comfortable doing it, he said fuck it. He really is a good man and I'm gonna do everything in my power to win him back. When I do, I promise to never, ever cheat on him again.

****

"What happened?" Mrs. Garcia asked the second the screen door unlocked. I guess my hair being all over the place and bags under my eyes were a dead giveaway. It also meant Kruz hadn't mentioned anything to her. It's good for me because I can spin this the way I want.

"He left me."

"Left you? I don't understand. Come in." She widened the screen and stepped aside for me to enter. Mr. Garcia sat at the kitchen table drinking his coffee. I spoke and he gave me the deadliest stare ever. It only meant he spoke to his son. They were very tight.

"Honey she said hello." Mrs. Garcia kissed his cheek and offered me a seat. As soon as I sat, he stood, grabbed his coffee and walked out.

"He's in one of his moods today. Tell me why my son left you." She sat there listening as I relayed my story and the what her son did a week ago.

"Why did you cheat on him if he gave you everything?"

"He cheated on me plenty of times."

"WHAT? My son isn't a cheater."

"I don't like going down on him so he goes out and get it from other women." Of course, I'm not gonna mention I allowed it.

"Oh hell no. My husband and I taught him better than that."

"I won't say it's revenge but it happened one time. I tried to apologize and say we can work it out but he's not listening. Then, I'm pregnant and..."

"Pregnant?"

"Yes and I didn't know until the morning he broke up with me. It's the reason I couldn't wait to get home and tell him."

"Does he know?"

"Yes."

"And he still doesn't want to be with you?" I let tears fall and that's all it took. She started cussing him out to me and couldn't wait to see her son. Kruz loves his mother and will do anything for her. I know once she gets in his ear, he'll be right back home.

"Go on home honey and get some rest." She stood and hugged me.

"Make sure you take care of my grand baby and I'll be speaking with my son soon."

"Ok and can you let him know how sorry I am. Maybe we can do counseling or something." She nodded with a smile on her face.

I got in my car and waved goodbye. Yea, my man is coming home and I'll be waiting with open arms.

"Ma, you just gonna take her side before hearing mine?" I listened to my boy speak to his mother on the phone about the shit with Zahra.

We were leaving a meeting that just put us on top of the food chain. We weren't the connect but if you needed to be supplied with anything you had no choice but to go through us. It didn't matter if it were weed, dope, crack, OxyContin, methadone, heroine or any other drug out there. In order to sell it, you had to clear it with us and we got a percentage.

It wasn't an easy job getting this top spot but me and him put in a lotta work to get here. That and another factor played in on us being here but no need to discuss it right now. We still had to be on top of shit to make sure no one fucked up.

Oh, my name is Kenron but the streets call me Jamaica because its where my parents are from. I'm the youngest of eight and probably the craziest. My pops always said he'd knew one of his kids would be like him and it was me. See, he's the reason Kruz and I are in the position we're in.

His best friend had a small empire, that over the years escalated. My dad had nothing to do with the drug part of it but helped keeps the books in order. Both of them tried to hand it over to me at the tender age of sixteen and I refused, unless Kruz did it with me. Some people claim brotherhood because they've hung with someone since diapers, and its exactly how he and I were. The only difference is, I trusted that nigga with my life and vice versa.

Over the years, we've been in fights, shootouts, robberies, and a bunch of other shit. We both did two years in juvie and during that time, I think we became closer. If you don't know, jails have gangs, and clicks.

The two of us stayed to ourselves until the white supremist group tried us. They thought since we were loners it was ok to try us. Let's just say, they tried it once and never did again. We gained even more respect behind those walls and niggas were feenin to be down with us. To this day, we still had about ten of those dudes on our team. They may not be as tight as Kruz and I, but they loyal as fuck.

Anyway, I'm 26, with money to last a lifetime, endless bitches and no crazy ass exes. I've had girlfriends growing up, however; I've never been in that deep kinda love like Kruz was. I felt bad for my nigga because he really did love Zahra. He told me how he wanted to marry her and have kids.

Now she's claiming to be pregnant and he's taking it hard for two reasons. One... he's not sure if it's his. And two...he never wanted to raise his kids in separate households.

He was a savage in these streets but a hopeless romantic behind closed doors with her. I always clowned him over it and he told me one day, I'll be the same. *Not gonna happen.*

"You good?" I parked at the diner. We had the team meet us here to celebrate making more money.

"Yea. Zahra told her she only cheated once. She mentioned the pregnancy and you know how my mom feels about that."

"What you gonna do?" He placed his phone in the clip.

"Nothing right now. I'm not taking her back and if that's my kid, we can co-parent."

31

"Damn, you really done with her?" I was shocked because they were my Beyoncé and Jay-Z couple.

"Yea. Who's to say it won't happen again? Not only that, I don't wanna get my dick sucked from anyone but my girl. I get she didn't wanna do it, but who offers their nigga to go outside their relationship?" My mind was blown when he told me she said that.

"I may not have been in love like you but any chick I fucked with ain't about to let another bitch suck me off."

"EXACTLY! It makes me think she's been dipping out longer than she says." I nodded and stepped in the diner behind him. It was after nine and not too many people were here. The waitress led us to the section I called for on the way.

"Hey y'all." One of the waitresses spoke, even though she was at a different table. Thirsty as hell for no reason. Two chicks walked in and I noticed the way Kruz stared at one of them. She was very pretty and I've seen her before because she's best friends with this chick I messed with.

"Who is she?" He asked and pointed to her.

"Go ask." I didn't know her name but I'd ask later if he really wanted me to.

"Nah. I'm only tryna fuck and she don't look like the type. Her face is turned up and I really don't feel like blacking out right now." I laughed because he will definitely curse a bitch out and dare her to battle him.

"A'ight y'all. After we order, we'll get to business." He said and everyone shook their heads. The waitress took all of our orders and Kruz discussed all the new details.

He was smart as hell in the business aspect of our job, where I did better handling the supplying, making sure the shit was delivered on time and all that. However; when it came to killing motherfuckers; we both got that shit on lock

We were now going to use a trucking company and airline to transport drugs. The head of the FAA had a serious drug problem and made a deal with the devil. We added him to the CIA, DEA, FBI and other law enforcements we employed. We were about to live the life and so was our team. Our motto is, *never leave anyone behind because they'll be the ones who'll turn on you and try to destroy everything.*

After the meeting, we all dispersed and drove to the strip club. My nigga needed to release some stress and there's nothing but pussy in a place like that. Plus, the bitches have been stalking him since hearing about the break-up. No idea who let it be known, but Zahra messed up big time because Kruz has always been in high demand. You know women fight hard for a taken man. And even harder when he's not; in hopes to get that wifey spot.

****

"Shit ma. You working the hell outta them jaws." I stared down at this shorty I've been fucking lately. Her pussy is A1 and so are her head skills. Yea, good pussy comes a dime a dozen but her shit is addictive. It's so good, I locked it down a while ago. We may not be a couple but she knows what the fuck it is.

"Jam, I wanna taste you." She gave me some stupid nickname but my ass loved hearing her say it.

"Take it." I blew the weed smoke in the air and watched her bring me to endless gratification. I swear she's the only woman who can make me cum a lot and hard.

"Shit woman." She kissed the top of my thighs, my stomach and chest. She knew I loved her doing it. She placed herself in front of me, removed the belt from her robe and revealed her exposed body. Shorty's body was bad as hell and if I didn't know her, I'd think she had work done.

I put my hands on her legs and slid them up and down her body. I licked two of my fingers, slid them in her folds and then inside. Her pussy clung to them as she pretended fucking them like they were my dick. She bit down on her lip and lifted her leg on the side of me. I placed my head in between her thighs, moved my tongue in further and lapped up all her juices.

She is the only woman I ever put my mouth on and its only because I knew she wasn't fucking no one else. Plus, I was her first sexual experience and dared her to fuck another nigga.

"Just like that K." I tasted more juices in my mouth.

"Oh shit Kenron. Yes baby." She threaded both hands in my hair and arched her back. When she did this, I knew a big one was coming and had to hold her tight to keep from falling over.

"Yessssssss." I grabbed her waist and watched her experience another gut-wrenching orgasm.

"We're not done." I scooted back on the bed, mounted her on top and closed my eyes. She by far could take me out in the bedroom in no time. That's how good her pussy was.

"Kenron, you feel so good. Mmmmmm. I'm gonna cum again." I opened my eyes and witnessed her do exactly what she said.

"Keep riding ma." She instructed me to sit against the headboard, turned in the cowgirl position, grabbed my legs and rode me so good, I fucked up and came inside. We usually use condoms or I pull out if we forget.

"K, I came in you."

"I know." Her breathing started slowing down.

"You still have the pills in the bathroom?" She asked about the extra Plan B's I kept at the house.

She's the only woman besides my family who's been here and has a key. Most men invite every woman they fuck with to their spot but not me. You can't have peace when too many bitches know where you lay your head.

"Yea." I gave her attitude and I'm not sure why.

"You ok?" She climbed on top and pecked my lips.

"Yup." I wasted no time stroking my man to get hard again. Since we fucked up, I may as well continue feeling her walls, raw.

After we finished and she was asleep, I pulled the covers over her and checked my messages like I did every night before I went to bed. I never wanted to go to sleep with them on my phone for some reason.

A few were from my boys and others were from the bitches I fucked here and there. One came with a video message and I must say, shorty did her thing without me. I found her number in my phone and hit her up. I probably should've waited until the morning but K is sleep. It's not like we're a couple so I'm not disrespecting her.

"Hey sexy. I see you got my message." Blue had one of those phone sex operator voices. She could have you whip your dick out and cum over the phone off that alone.

"I got it but why you doing it while I'm not there?" I went in the kitchen to grab something to drink.

"I tried waiting but you didn't answer. You know when I'm horny, I have to do my thing."

"I do know." I smiled, twisted the cap off the water and took a sip.

"What's up for tomorrow?" I questioned because K had to work overnight. We didn't fuck all the time but she did stay over a lot. If I knew she was going to stay with me, I'd never sleep with a woman and come here to her, just in case she wanted to fuck.

"You tell me." I was thinking and told her I'll let her know.

"I'll see you in the morning or whenever you get here."

"You got that. Keep that pussy wet for me." I heard someone clear their throat and turned to see K crying.

"I'll hit you back." I hung the phone up and placed it on the counter.

"What's wrong?" I noticed she was dressed, had the purse on her shoulder and keys in her hand.

38

"My phone rang and it was Rhythm asking me to come get her. I searched the room for you to say I'd be back and you weren't there. I figured you were down here grabbing something to drink so I put my clothes on and came to say goodbye. Imagine my surprise to hear you making plans to fuck another bitch."

"K." She put her hand up.

"Before you say it, I'm well aware we're not a couple and you're free to do whatever. I walked into this fuck buddy thing with my eyes open; knowing you'd continue bedding other women." I could tell how hurt she was.

"You couldn't wait for me to leave Jamaica? I mean, am I that bad in bed you had to make plans to be with another woman less than 24 hours of having me?"

"K, you know it's not like that." I tried to move closer, but each step I took she backed away.

"It's not, says the man telling a woman to keep her pussy wet. Is this what you do when I go to sleep?"

"Nah. She sent me a message and fuck! I shouldn't have called her back. I'm sorry K."

"Jamaica, I'm not comfortable with this arrangement anymore. We can be friends and..." I never gave her the chance to finish because my hand was wrapped around her throat. The thought of her leaving me alone made me snap.

"I don't care what you want. You better be in my bed tonight and every night like you've been doing."

WHAP! She smacked the fuck outta me. If this were anyone else, I would've already ended them.

"The moment you put your hands around my neck only verified we don't need to be together.

"Shit! I'm sorry K. Let me make it up to you."

"Goodbye Jamaica." She went to open the door, turned to me and shook her head. I knew we were done and it was killing me.

"K, we are never gonna be over."

"You don't scare me Jamaica and you know why?" She placed her hand on the side of my face.

"Because inside that cold heart of yours, I know there's love for me." I stayed silent because she's right. I did have strong feelings for her. I wiped the tears falling from her eyes. I knew she was in love with me because she's voiced it plenty of times. I just never reciprocated the feelings I had.

"Too bad your dick makes all your decisions. Goodbye." She hopped in her car and sped out my driveway.

I wiped the tears running down my face, and tried paying attention to the road but it was hard when I was currently suffering a heartbreak. Like I told Jamaica, I'm aware we weren't a couple and how he slept with other women. I'm not upset about that as much as I am with him calling a woman right after we had sex. Yes, he was my first and showed me everything in the bedroom but am I horrible? It has to be mediocre for him to look elsewhere.

Am I in love with him? Absolutely! Do I deserve better? Of course, but when your heart is with someone, it's not easy tearing yourself away. No, my self-esteem isn't low and I can get men but I wanted him. I assumed being under him all the time, sexing him like crazy and revealing my feelings for him would make him see, I'm the one.

I was fooling myself, knowing bitches threw themselves at him and Kruz. The difference is, his boy never took the bait, where he slung his dick any and everywhere.

People didn't know about us and it hurt like hell listening to women discuss wanting or even being with him

42

while we were out. It's like the whole fucking town slept with him. If women saw us together, they'd still approach him because they only looked at me as Zahra's sister and he must've been helping me with something.

He never disrespected me in public and would tell them to beat it but I'm sure he hooked up with them at a later date. I do know after tonight, I refuse to waste any more time with him. If I need sex, I'll do myself or find someone who isn't afraid of him. I can't continue loving a man who won't commit or even express his feelings for me.

I parked in front of Rhythm's house, pulled the visor down and tried to fix my face. It was no use because the tears wouldn't stop falling. I don't know why I allowed this secret relationship to go on for two years without putting my foot down. The only people who knew about us were Kruz and Rhythm.

I should've known after a year he wouldn't commit but following my heart, I stayed and now look. I'm sitting in front of my best friend's house looking pathetic and trying my hardest not to answer Jamaica, who has rung my phone back to back since I pulled off.

"OH, HELL NO! WHAT DID HE DO?" Rhythm came out barking when she saw my face. She didn't even know what happened and was ready to fight. I got out the car and hugged her tight. I loved this chick as if she came from my mother's womb. Blood couldn't make us more related.

"Can we go in?" She closed the car door and looped her arm in mine as we stepped inside.

"TiTi!" My six-year-old Godson/ nephew Axel, called out and ran to me.

"What are you doing up lil man? Its late." I glanced at Rhythm who was putting her shoes on.

"I'm sick."

"What's wrong?"

"That's why I called you. My car broke down and I think he has an ear infection. His fever is going up and I'm nervous. Can you take us?"

"Let's go." I picked him up, while Rhythm grabbed their things and locked the door. We both stopped and glanced at the dudes across the street at the motel where we worked. They were outside smoking weed as usual in front of the room.

"I bet its two." I told her referencing to how many chicks a piece they had in there.

"Two men. I would say three or four because they're greedy and probably switch up." I sat Axel in the backseat and placed his seatbelt on.

"True." We always tried to take bets on people who would rent a room.

"How many times?" I asked about my phone she picked up.

"DAMN! Bitch, he called fifty-six times." She turned the phone to me so I could see.

"Ooooh mommy. No cursing." We started laughing.

"I'm sorry sweetie." I asked her to cut the phone off and just as she went to do it, there was a bang on my window.

"Get out!" I sucked my teeth. This motherfucker must've tracked my damn phone.

"My nephew is sick. I'm taking him to the ER."

"Rhythm can take him. Let's go!" He snatched the door open and helped me get out.

"TiTi, you not coming?" I heard and watched as Rhythm walked over to the driver's side.

"Sis, I promise I'd stay with you but he needs to go."

"I'm fine sis. Call me when you're done." She gave me a hug and mean mugged Jamaica.

"Don't put your hands on her." He snapped his neck at me. I guess he assumed she knew what he did.

"Love you Axel."

"Love you too auntie." He blew me a kiss and I used my phone to call an Uber. Jamaica had no reason to be here and I don't plan on staying.

"I'm sorry Kalila." I rolled my eyes and sat on the porch. Rhythm stayed in a two-family house with her son. Her landlord stayed on one side and she on the other with Axel. She was trying to find something smaller because the rent was too high, which is why she always worked overtime. She refused to be homeless and I don't blame her.

"Go home Jamaica. Don't you have to get ready for your fuck buddy in the morning?"

"K, what do you want from me?"

"Nothing Kenron. Not a fucking thing." He hated when I cursed but he should know I only did it when someone pissed me off.

"Are you gonna say something?" He stood in front of me.

"What do you want me to say Jam, huh?" I always went back and forth calling him both names.

"Am I hurt? Yes. Do I still love you? Yes. Will I get over it? Eventually. You can go now."

"Why do you love me Kalila?"

"What?" He caught me off guard with the question. He lifted my face and made me look at him.

"Why do you love me?"

"I love everything about you Kenron." He smiled when I called him that.

"I love how you make love to me and then hold me all night. I love how when we go out of the country on vacations,

47

you treat me like I'm the only woman in the world. I love the talks we have about having a future together. I love how gentle you are with my feelings, and knowing you're with other women, you never try to hurt me. You keep that and your street life away from me to make sure I have a smile on my face but you fucked up Kenron." His smile disappeared.

"I…" He couldn't even say the words and that hurt. We talk about any and everything, yet; he couldn't say those three words to me.

"Don't worry about it baby. You may not say it, but I know how you feel. Well I thought I did." I stepped off Rhythm's porch when the Uber pulled up. I turned around and walked over to him. He wiped the tears falling down my face and hugged me. I pushed him off and got myself together.

"Just know that as long as I live, you and only you, will always be first love. I love you Kenron. Goodnight." I kissed his lips and ran to the car. I could hear him calling my name, yet; I refused to turn around because I may go back to him.

I asked the driver to pull off and went home. I didn't have to worry about him stopping by because again, no one knew about us and since I live in the center of the hood, he'd never pop up. I didn't live in the projects but I may as well have. Shit, my house is directly across the street.

****

"Here girl." My mom shouted and threw the house phone at me.

"Ouch ma." I hadn't even opened my eyes yet and here she is throwing phones at me.

"Hurry up and get yo ass up. Its Saturday and we got cleaning to do." She went to leave and turned around.

"Oh. Somebody sent yo dirty ass some flowers." She smiled and told me I must've turned some nigga out.

"Bye ma." I hated she talked shit first and then said something nice at the end.

"Hello."

"Hey TiTi."

"Axel. How are you feeling honey?" I hadn't spoken to him in a few days. The night Rhythm took him to the doctors they kept him overnight. They diagnosed him with an ear and sinus infection, gave him antibiotics and said he needed to rest.

I planned on stopping by but I ended up covering her shift at work and was tired as fuck.

"I'm ok. Mommy said we're coming over in a little while. Are you awake?"

"Yea. Let me speak to mommy." He passed the phone.

"How long does he have to be on the medicine?"

"Until it runs out. I tried to get him to stay home at least one more day but as you can tell, his ass ain't listening. Do you know he woke up asking if you were ok because the big scary guy was still there when we left?" I busted out laughing and went downstairs to see who delivered me flowers.

"Here's the card." My mom handed it to me.

"Ugh, why did you take it out the flowers?"

"You need to be happy. Your pregnant ass sister almost read it and we both know whoever you fucking is a secret. She'd probably blast it to everyone if she knew who."

"Did your mom just say Zahra's pregnant?"

"Girl yes. Hurry up and get over here so we can grill my mom."

"Y'all ain't grilling shit and tell Rhythm to bring my grandson over here. Got him sick and shit." She started laughing. My mom loved Rhythm the same as I.

"Well?"

"Well what?" I snapped on Zahra who stepped in from off the back-porch half dressed.

"Who are the flowers from? Must be one of these knuckleheads out here." I waved her off and strolled in the living room. I opened the card and covered my mouth.

Kalila, I'm so fucking sorry baby. I never meant to hurt you. I'm going half-crazy right now because you won't answer my calls or texts. I miss you K. Call me. I placed the card against my heart and leaned on the window smiling. I appreciated the gesture but he still hasn't told me those three words to my face and he probably won't.

I've been around him long enough to know he's too hard core to let a woman know how he feels. He thinks people will find him weak if he shows emotions. I told him many times it's not true but he lives by it. You can't make someone see what they don't want to.

"Damn, he got you smiling hard."

"Whatever." I ran upstairs to shower and turned my phone on. There were tons of messages from him. I could've responded but nope. Let him sweat. If he really wants me, I'll make his ass work for it.

I went downstairs after getting dressed and started helping my mom clean the house. The music was blasting, you could smell the incense burning and hear her singing. My mom is old school so when *Fools Paradise by Melissa Morgan* came on, she was in her glory. I grabbed the broom and stood next to her in the mirror.

I'm taking out this time. To give you a piece of my mind. Who do you think you are? Maybe, one day you'll be a star, until then baby, I'm the one who's crazy, cuz it's the way, you make me feel.

There was a knock on the screen and both of us looked. Rhythm came in, took her phone out and used it as a microphone. All three of us swore we were getting it. Axel, had my hands in his as we danced around the living room. Zahra stepped in and turned the music down. All of us stared at her.

"What? This baby has me sleepy and I can't with y'all hollering like wolves." She plopped down on the couch.

"You tried it heffa. Either get yo ass up to help clean or go home and sleep." My mother told her and handed the Clorox wipes to her. She blew her breath and stormed out the door.

"Where did I go wrong with that chile?" My mother went in the kitchen and grabbed a soda.

"Nanny, I'm thirsty too." My mom gave him some of her soda and sat him on her lap. My mother was the second mom to Rhythm and if she could've adopted her, she would have. Her mom is around, they just don't fuck with each other on that level.

"Your sister is about to have a child with a man who doesn't want her."

"Axel, let me turn some cartoons on for you." I took him out and sat him in the living room. I placed a blanket on him and locked the front door.

"Why is he out Rhythm?"

"Ma, I tried to keep him in but he was worried about this heffa leaving with the big scary guy."

"Whatever. Anyway, why doesn't Kruz want the baby?" I bypassed the conversation so my mother wouldn't ask me who the guys was. I'm not about to tell anyone who he is, when he's unsure about how he feels.

"Would you?" I gave my mother the side eye.

"I know all about your sister being a whore. Shit, the entire hood knows."

"What? How?"

"I guess Kruz went out and people saw him leave with different women. We all know he wouldn't cheat on her. Someone asked if he had a woman and he told them, and I quote what Stacey said." Stacey is the nosy neighbor who kept my mom informed.

"I'll never make that ho, my woman again."

54

"WHATTTTTTT?" Rhythm and I shouted out. We were shocked because he worshipped the ground my sister walked on. I'm not saying they didn't have issues because every couple does but he loved the shit outta Zahra.

"Yup. Anyway, she's about two months and his mother called asking did I wanna help set up a damn baby shower." It's no secret my mom could care less about her. She felt his mom stayed in their business too much and I agree.

"Enough talk about her. Kalila, I've been meaning to talk to you." I could hear the sadness in her voice.

"What's wrong?"

"They're going up on the mortgage again and I can't afford it. We're gonna have to move into a one bedroom or in the projects."

"The projects?"

"Yes, and the head of housing said he can get us over there in two weeks." I was pissed because my grandparents raised my mother in this house. It's been in the family for years. Not to mention, she just got brand new siding on it and renovated the entire downstairs. When I got a better job, we were gonna do the upstairs.

"Ma, why didn't you tell me?"

"You just graduated college and I didn't wanna put no stress on you to work."

"Ma, I work part time at the motel."

"I know but it's not the job you went to school for." I went to the community college and worked on the side to keep money in my pocket. My mom did tell me to take a break for the summer but I didn't listen.

"I'll start sending more applications out." I sent a few out but nothing major because honestly, I didn't wanna work in the corporate world yet.

"It's ok honey. As long as we have a roof over our head, we'll be fine."

"What about Zahra?"

"Please." She waved her hand in the air.

"Don't tell me she said no." I saw a tear coming down my mother's face and wanted to go beat my sister's ass.

"She is about to have a baby now and doesn't have it."

"Ma, I've seen her account. Kruz gave her tons of money. There's at least two million in there." This is another reason I hated my sister. She is selfish as fuck when it came to family but outsiders could get the clothes off her back if needed. Kruz adored her and kept her laced in all the expensive shit. Kept her bank account full and let her drive in the most expensive whips.

"Ma, you can stay with me and Axel. Matter of fact, we can move here and I can help you with the mortgage." And this is why I loved Rhythm.

"I can't ask you to uproot Axel like that."

"Why not? He loves coming here and I'm sure he'll have no problem waking up to his favorite nanny everyday." My mom started crying harder and both of us hugged her.

"Are you sure Rhythm. I don't want to get rid of this place but I don't want to put you out either."

"I don't mind. Big Axel helps a lot with his son and I hate living across from the motel anyway." She shrugged and sat down across from my mom.

"Do you have the mortgage for this month? I mean is it already paid?" My mom nodded her head yes.

"Ok. I'll give my landlord a thirty-day notice. I'll be out before then but he can at least place an ad in the paper."

"I love you girls so much."

"We love you too." I hated seeing my mom cry. I ran upstairs and grabbed my bank card.

"Here." I handed it to her.

"What's this?"

"It's my bank card and you're a co-applicant. It's about ten thousand on it and…"

"Ten thousand dollars?" They both asked at the same time.

"Yes. I saved my school checks and my secret admirer gave me money. I never spent it and put it in an account. There's about seventy in the savings account."

"Seventy dollars?" I gave both of them a look.

"Seventy thousand."

"Oh my God Kalila. You better not be selling your body."

"I only sold it to him." She sucked her teeth.

"He was my first ma and I'm in love with him. He's just stuck on having multiple women and I stayed around knowing this, so don't flip out."

"It doesn't explain why he gave you this kind of money."

"Anytime we would go away on vacation or he'd go away for business, he'd give me money to buy whatever I want. I thought he loved me but I think he's tryna keep me from being with someone else."

"Kalila, you know just like I do how much he loves you." Rhythm said and she's right. I do know but until he says it out his own mouth, it is what it is.

"Yea well, his love needs to be shown because what he's doing ain't it." She rolled her eyes.

"Anyway, mommy pay off what you can towards the mortgage and we can go from there." The only reason why she even had a mortgage is because she took equity out to fix the house up and it wasn't cheap.

"Kalila this is your money."

"Ma, this is our money. Take it and tell me how much more you need."

"Kalila."

"It's fine mommy. Let me help you." She nodded and hugged both of us again. She went in the living room, picked Axel up and took him in her room.

"Let's smoke." Rhythm, grabbed my hand and we sat on the front porch rolling up.

"Looks like we'll be living like sisters now." She finished rolling and lit the blunt. I stared at her and smiled.

"Yup and we're going out to celebrate." She laughed and passed me the blunt. I had to come up with a plan and fast. My mother did not need to stress herself over bullshit. I hope karma gets my sister because she damn sure deserves it.

"We about to shut the club down." Kalila said when we stepped out. We both had on bodycon dresses with strap up heels. I borrowed some from her because Jamaica definitely laced her with nice shit. She did our hair and I did the makeup.

In high school we tried our hands in cosmetology and loved it. We did girls hair and makeup for prom, eight grade dances and anything else they'd ask for. It was a hustle but we didn't make a lotta money off it, therefore; we had regular jobs. We still have people call us during prom time though.

"Girl, I just wanna have a few drinks and dance." The line wasn't that long but it was hot out and no one wanted to stand here.

"We're about to find us some men." I told her and we looked at each other before falling in a fit of laughter. I had no one at the moment and she had a man afraid to commit.

Axel was the last and only man I've ever been with. We were perfect together until three years ago. His attitude changed and so did the way he treated me. It didn't start until he made a little bit of money. Isn't that always how it goes with men? It's not like he sold drugs and had mad money. His dad owned a car lot and he worked there all through school. I guess any money, is better than no money.

He and I were middle school sweethearts and each other's first sexual experience. You couldn't tell us nothing about the other and we were already married in our heads with kids and a house. No relationship is perfect so of course, once we made it to the high school, the chicks became more aggressive. I can't tell you how many arguments I've gotten into over him.

I'm not a fighter but I will if need be. I never wanna be brought outta character and it seems like the chicks would do it on purpose. Axel would address each chick and let them know, never to say anything to me but it would go in one ear and out the other with them.

When I found out about our son in my junior year, he promised to do better and get us a place. I admit he did get us a spot where I'm at now, but over the years all we did was argue and fight. It got to a point where we slept in different rooms and I only saw him in passing.

62

Now he stays in a big ass house with his new girlfriend, Caroline. She's expecting their second child and the two of us never say more than hello to one another. I don't have a problem with her and as long as my son doesn't come home stating she treated him wrong, I'm good.

I felt bad for her because every time he comes to get my son, he tells me he'll leave her if I take him back. I'd never put myself back in the same situation. He'll never come home to me and go say the same words to her when picking up their kids.

His mom is no better because she always says I'm the one who got away and no other woman will be good enough for him. She's even said it in front of Caroline.

"Next." Security shouted and stared at Kalila.

"Why you standing in line?"

"I don't need special privileges."

"You better not tell him I let you stand in line." She waved him off as he passed us our ID's. For someone who didn't claim Kalila, he made sure she didn't have to stand in line.

We stepped in and the music was blasting. People were everywhere and the bar was packed. Women were barely dressed and men lined the wall with drinks in their hands. You could see them watching and preying on who they'd try and take home.

People were on the dance floor getting down too. The entire vibe was cool and I couldn't wait to get a few drinks in my system and feel the same.

"Let's grab that table." Kalila pointed to one these women just left. We took a seat and there were no waitresses in sight.

"Stay here. I'll go get drinks. I don't want anyone taking our seats."

"They won't because I'll be here." I turned and saw Zahra walk up with some chick she called her friend. I ain't never seen her before but who knows with Zahra?

"Who said we wanted you here?" I heard Kalila ask when I walked off. I pushed my way through the crowd and found a spot at the bar. I leaned in to ask for our drinks and someone stood next to me. I didn't pay the person any mind.

"Can I get two screw drivers and Malibu Bay Breezes."

"Sure. And you?" She pointed to the guy next to me and I turned to stare at one of the most gorgeous men I've ever seen. He was beautiful if I must say so myself. His swag was on point and if I were a ho, I'd fuck him in the bathroom right now.

"Send the waitress to VIP with two bottles of Ace of Spades, Titos and Henney."

"Damn." I said to myself and he must've read my lips.

"Damn what?" His eyes roamed my body and he had to be impressed because he licked his lips.

"Ummmm. I… was just…. ugh… nothing." I turned my head and slid down a little. His cologne was taking over my nostrils.

"Yo! Put lil mama's drink on my tab."

"Oh no. That's ok." I grabbed the two twenties' out my clutch and placed them in his pocket. He grabbed my wrist and put his mouth by my ear.

"Never put your hand in a nigga's pocket and save your money. I'm sure you need it." I caught an attitude quick.

"What? You think because you brought all these drinks it's supposed to impress me."

"Not really because I don't give a fuck if it does or not. I saw you sweating me, so I decided to buy your drinks." My mouth fell open.

"Sweating you?" He smirked because he knew just like I did, how handsome he was. However; he didn't have to be so got damn arrogant.

"You buying a few drinks don't impress me." The bartender placed the drinks on the counter.

"Yo, let shorty pay for her own shit since she's tryna show her independence. Peace." He hit me with the two fingers and stepped off.

"That'll be fifty-two."

"Fifty-two dollars for four drinks?"

"Honey you're not in a cheap club."

"That means?"

"It means you have to purchase a bottle of something. Since you didn't, I gave you the cheapest thing on the menu; red wine." She placed it on the counter.

"There should be a sign up." She pointed behind her and there it was. I took the drinks and asked her to watch the other ones until I returned. I couldn't take them all at once.

"Hey!" She shouted and had me lean over the bar to hear her.

"Next time you see that man, try not to get smart. He's not the type to let shit go."

"What is he a gangster or something?"

"Nah. More like a savage who don't give a fuck about killing you or your family in front of you." She shrugged her shoulders.

"Oh. Thanks for the warning." She winked and walked off to help another customer.

I glanced around the bar for the VIP section. I'm assuming it was on the second floor because security stood in front of the door. Women were up there stripping on the pole that was visible to anyone looking. I shook my head at the men smacking their asses and throwing money.

"Who you staring at?" Kalila asked and took the drinks from me.

"No one. I'm gonna run to the bathroom."

"Good. Stay away longer if you don't mind." I gave Zahra the finger and kept it moving.

It was hectic getting in the bathroom and the women weren't even using it. I sucked my teeth and pushed passed them in the mirror. I never understood why women spent more time in here than in the club. I stepped out and ran into a hard chest.

"Not only did you insult me at the bar, you run into me." Panic struck after hearing what the bartender told me. I've been around wanna be savages and never took them seriously but the way the bartender described him, he's not someone I should take lightly.

"Oh my God. I'm so sorry. Please don't kill me."

"What?"

"The bartender said you're a savage and I better watch myself. Look. I got a son and he needs me. If you want me to leave, I can. Shit. I'm sorry for running into you."

"You good. What's up though?"

"Huh?" I was confused as to what he asked.

"You tryna satisfy my need tonight?"

"Pahahahahaha." I laughed in his face.

"It's funny?" He slid his tongue across his teeth.

"No disrespect but hell yea it is. I'm sure you have women at your beckon call but I'm not that type of girl." He went to speak and I stopped him.

"Before you say all women say that, I'm not all women and I mean what I say. Have a good night." I moved past and thought he'd stop me but he didn't.

I made my way back to the seat and felt someone pull my arm. I saw Kalila's face and her sisters.

"What in the hell?"

"Let me talk to you real quick." The same guy from the bar and bathroom, gripped my arm and pushed me forward.

"Why you grabbing on her?" Zahra stood and he told her to sit the fuck down.

"Ummm excuse us." He literally used me as a shield to move people out the way. I was embarrassed and the look of shock appeared on people's face. I glanced at the bartender and she was shaking her head.

When we stepped outside, someone pulled a black Tahoe with tinted windows in front of us. Instead of asking me nicely to get in, he pushed me in and told the driver to go around the corner. Hell yea, I was scared.

"Now, what's up?" The truck stopped and the street was dark as hell. I placed my back against the door and ignored him.

"Oh yea." He smirked, got out the car and I felt my body about to fall out. I almost hit the ground, had he not saved me.

"What in the fuck is wrong with you?"

"Oh, you one of those ratchet chicks?"

"No, I'm not."

"I can't tell."

"You don't have to tell anything but if you must know, I try not to curse because of my son but sometimes people make you." I gave him a fake smile.

"And I don't appreciate you dragging me out a club, yanking me out the truck and making assumptions." I pulled my dress down and turned to look in the window to make sure my hair was ok.

"What the heck is so important that I was dragged out here anyway? You said enough inside." I crossed my arms.

"Who are you?"

"Are you serious right now?"

"Yup. I know every bitch in town and I've never seen you before." I rolled my eyes at him calling women bitches.

"Look, whatever your name is. You don't know me because I don't come out a lot. I mind my own business, take care of my son and stay outta the streets. And you really shouldn't refer to all women as bitches. It's not very gentlemen like." He gave me a weird stare.

"What?" I shifted my weight to my left and put my hands on my hips.

"Your name?"

"Huh?"

"What the fuck is your name?"

"Did anyone ever teach you how to speak to a woman?" He chuckled.

"My name is Rhythm."

"Rhythm? Like rhythm, and blues?"

"Ha ha ha ha. Very funny but yes. I don't know why my mother named me that before you ask."

"Well Rhythm you intrigue me and that fact you have no idea who I am and still popped shit, has me interested."

"Too bad. Your first impression was horrible and I don't think I'd want a volatile man like you around my son."

"I'm just tryna fuck, not be a stepdaddy."

"Ughhhhhh. Take me back."

"Where you stay?"

"No need to give you my address because you won't be stopping by. My pussy isn't up for sale. Sorry." I shrugged and opened the door.

"Pussy comes a dime a dozen ma and trust you ain't all that." I was offended. Not only did he pull me out the club but insulted me for no reason.

"Then it's no problem not exchanging numbers."

"Sure ain't." He moved me out the way, hopped in the truck and rolled the window down.

"It shouldn't be a problem with you walking yo smart ass back to the club. Peace."

"You mother…"

"Ahh ugh. You said, you don't curse." He started laughing. I stormed off in the direction of the club. It literally was around the corner. I came strolling in front of the club and Kalila ran over. She began checking me over and asking if he hurt me.

"Do you know who that is?"

"No and I don't want to. He's rude as fuck and…" I stopped speaking when he walked out with two chicks on the side of him. He looked at me and winked. I flipped him the bird and he pretended to come for me. I jumped behind Kalila and she thought the shit was hysterical. Zahra on the other hand, had an attitude and I could tell she was upset over something.

"Let's go bitch so I can fill you in." Kalila snatched my hand and we walked fast to her car.

"Who in this black truck and why they stopped next to my car?"

"Who knows?" I said and stared down at my phone before it was ripped out my hand. I looked up and it was the same guy.

"You are rude as hell."

"I know."

"What do you even want with a woman who isn't all that?" I put in air quotes and he ignored me. He did something to my phone and tossed it in my lap.

"Answer when I fucking call."

"No thanks." He snatched the door open and pulled me out.

"Really sis? You gonna let him do this to me."

"I'm gonna let Kalila fill you in on who I am but let's get one thing straight." I rolled my eyes.

"That mouth is gonna get you in a world of trouble." I hated that his aggressiveness had me wet as hell.

"I hate to be a bearer of bad news but my panties are showing because you have my dress up." He looked down and licked his lips.

"Let that be the last time anyone see this." He smacked me on the ass and hopped back in the truck.

"Answer the fucking phone when I call." He rolled the window up and the truck sped off. I slammed the car door and locked it so he couldn't re open it, if he decided to bring his ass back around. I turned to Kalila who was hysterical by now.

"Who the hell is that?"

"Girl, I need you to tell me how you got that nigga claiming you already. Did you fuck him in the truck?"

"What? Hell no!"

"Bitch, that's Kruz."

"Kruz who? Not the Kruz your sister just broke up with." I knew Zahra was with him for a long time but as crazy as it may seem, she never brought him around us. I think Kalila and her mom only met him if he picked her up and even then, he waved from the car. The bitch definitely didn't want anyone to see him and I can see why.

"Yup and trust me, she's gonna be asking mad questions."

"She can ask all she wants. You know damn well I'm not tryna deal with no one she has. She seems like the bitter ex who would get on someone's nerves."

"We'll see what he says. And by the looks of things, I'd say he's definitely gonna call so you better answer." I gave her the finger and laid my head on the seat as she drove us home. Kruz is fine as shit, but I'm not tryna deal with Zahra or any other woman regarding him. He can keep those problems.

"Bro. You never told me Kalila had another sister."

Jamaica and I were sitting in my office going over paperwork. The new deal required us to be on top of everything. We were doing shit most dealers only dreamed about.

"The only sister I know of is Zahra."

"Not that bitch. I'm talking about Rhythm." He smirked.

"What?"

"They've been best friends since kids. When you see her?" I thought about her little feisty ass the night at the club.

She's definitely shorter than me and stood at five foot five. Her thighs are thick and she had a little junk in her trunk. Her chest wasn't that big but suckable for sure. I could tell the long hair was hers by the way she kept swinging it without worrying if it would fall off. Let alone, I caught her head before she fell out the truck and didn't feel any braids. She had a dimple on the left side of her cheek and the little make up she had on, did nothing to accentuate how pretty she was.

I got a kick outta her little ass too. She had no clue who I was, which made my interest in her grow. Most woman wanted me for two reasons. One... to say they had me. And two... for money and respect. People can call me cocky all they want but the truth is, every woman dealing with a kingpin wants to sit on top. They want women to envy them. It's sad but it's a fact.

"I met her a few times but I'm not sure you're her type." He laughed.

"Nigga what you saying? I'm every bitch type."

"From the way Kalila described her, she's quiet, goes to work and minds her business. She's got a kid by the dude who works at the car lot. Both of them work at the motel we handle business at."

"No shit!" We've murked quite a bit of people at that hotel. We always had someone clean up and make it like nothing ever went down. Shit, we reserved the room for a year in advance just to handle our shit. We have a warehouse too but sometimes we don't feel like driving out there.

"Yea but shoot your shot."

"I'ma stop by later."

"Hold up. You got her address?" I shrugged my shoulders and went back to looking on my computer.

"Let me know how it goes."

"I don't have to. You're coming with me." He gave me the side eye.

"Stop acting like your ass ain't missing her friend."

"Whatever."

"You don't have to front for me. I know you love her."

"I'm not sure it's love."

"Trust me; it's love. Let's go." I shut my computer down and looked at the time. It was after eight. Shorty should still be at work.

"Where we going?"

"To the motel."

"Motel?"

"Yup! Shorty working until 11."

"Damn nigga. Let me find out you stalking."

"Not stalking just checking on an investment."

"Oh, she's an investment now?"

"Shut yo ass up and come on."

"How you know she working until 11?"

"Because as you were telling me our peoples was sending me her info." I laughed as he shook his head.

On the drive over, Zahra was blowing my phone up. I'm sure it's to question me about Rhythm. I saw her when I pulled shorty out the club. Her face was turned up and jealousy took over. I don't know why when she's never introduced the woman as her friend and we aren't together. If she wanted to keep a nigga, her legs should've stayed closed.

"I'll be right back." Jamaica lit a blunt and closed his eyes. I knew he was battling with telling Kalila he loved her. He didn't wanna make her his girl and mess up by cheating. I guess it don't matter because he messed up anyway. Couple or not, a woman doesn't wanna hear the guy she's messing with making plans with another after they just fucked.

****

"I'll be right there." I heard when I rung the bell.

The motel wasn't bad looking and yes this is my first time inside. I never got my hands dirty so if a person lost their

80

life here, I'd hear about it the following day. The only time I dealt with shit is when things spiraled outta control.

"Can I help you?" She sounded out of breath and came to the window in a pair of leggings and a sports bra. Sweat poured down the side of her face and in the middle of her chest.

"Yea. Come here." She folded her arms across her chest and smirked. I pushed the door open before she could lock it and went straight to the back. Wasn't shit back there but a small loveseat, TV, desk, computer and a bunch of keys. There was a treadmill off in the corner, which I'm assuming she just got off of.

"You are nosy and who said you could come in here?" I looked at her and shook my head.

"You leaving doors unlocked and I go wherever I feel like it." Her hair was up in a ponytail with some strands sticking to her face. I moved them out the way and stared at her lips.

"Ummm. What can I do for you?" She put space in between us.

"I wanna take you out."

81

"No thanks." She walked ahead of me and her small ass jiggled in those tight ass pants.

"Why not?"

"Your ex is my best friends' sister. Regardless if I like her or not, it's not right."

"Fuck her."

"Ugh you did and now the chick is crazy." She made both of us laugh.

"On some real shit, let me take you out. If the date is a disaster, you'll never hear from me again." I lifted her on the counter and she stared down at me.

"I don't know Kruz." I smiled listening to my name roll off her tongue.

"I'll pick you up Friday at eight. Dress nice."

"I didn't say yes."

"You don't have to." I pulled her in closer and separated her lips. Once my tongue entered, lust took over and we went at it like lovers.

"Mmmm. Shit. What am I doing?" She pushed me off and hopped off the counter.

"You're doing exactly what you want."

"And that is?"

"Tryna see if this nigga is worth it."

"But I..."

"You'll find out soon enough and if I think you're worth it, I'm about to take you on a whole nother level."

"Kruz." I pecked her lips, opened the door and walked out. I shouted for her to lock the door and I could see from the window she did.

"How'd it go?"

"Perfect. We got a date tomorrow." He nodded and asked me to drop him off at home.

****

Me: *Hey ma, I know we had a date tonight but my plans changed. I got you tomorrow.* I sent the message to Rhythm.

RNB: *Its ok. I have plans too. I forgot about them.*

Me: *It better not be with no nigga.*

RNB: *And if it were, its nothing you can do. You're not my man.* She sent me a laughing emoji with the tongue handing out.

Me: *Now that you're my investment all bets are off with any other nigga.*

RNB: *Investment? Whatever. I have to get ready. TTYL*

Me: *Don't play with me.*

She didn't respond and I was lowkey mad and I don't even know why. She ain't my girl, nor have I sampled the pussy. How in the hell am I feeling this chick already? Could it be I'm not tryna be alone?

I've been with Zahra so long, I'm not use to being by myself. Maybe I'll take a step back and keep her as a friend from a distance. But what if another nigga steps in and takes her? Shit! I had so much going on in my head, I didn't pay attention to this bitch pulled up behind me at my parents. I finally stopped by after avoiding my moms for a month and a half. Every time she asked me to stop by or call, I'd always say I was busy.

I knew where my mother stood when it came to raising a child under one roof. However; I'm not about to be unhappy tryna please her or Zahra. Do I still love Zahra? Of course, but she chose to cheat and that's on her. I'm not denying my involvement in being unfaithful either, and I didn't get my dick sucked as much as people may assume. Wrong is wrong and had she not volunteered me to do it, I wouldn't have.

I stepped out my truck, locked it and walked in the house. I could see out my peripheral this bitch had tears coming down her face and I'm not in the mood. I'm sure she made herself cry to get sympathy. She won't get it from me or my pops.

He and I were tight and he agreed that she needs to be outta my life. It's one thing to dip out but another to have a condom left in you and try to fuck someone else.

"You couldn't hold the door for me Kruz?" I heard and moved in the living room with my father. She was starting already and we've only been here thirty seconds.

"What up son?" I gave him a hug.

"Not much. I came to speak with ma, but it looks like I picked the wrong day." Zahra sucked her teeth and strolled in the kitchen.

"Son, she's been here almost everyday asking why you don't want her and the other bullshit. When your mom tries to get me to speak to you, I walk away. Ain't nobody got time for no ho's. Bad enough a ho about to raise my grandchild." I busted out laughing. He never bit his tongue.

"We don't even know if it's mine."

WHAP! I felt a smack on the back of my head.

"Boy, she made a mistake."

"Yea, a mistake that left a condom in her pussy. Yo, I'm out." I rose to my feet and towered over my mom who had a shocked look on her face.

"Kruz Arturo Garcia, you wait right there." I stopped at the screen door.

"What's this about you messing with some chick she's friends with?"

"First off, I don't mess with no chick she's friends with." I had no idea what the hell Zahra told my mother.

86

"Rhythm, Kruz." I smirked and walked up on her.

"You wanna know what's funny." I folded my arms across my chest in front of her.

"In the four years we've been together, I have never, ever heard you say this woman's name and now all of a sudden, you friends with her?" She backed away.

"I just met her the night at the club and I can admit she intrigues the fuck outta me. But let me put you up on something real quick." Zahra sucked her teeth.

"You tryna play this innocent role in front of my mother but you look stupid as fuck Zahra."

"What?"

"You saw me walk out that night with two bitches I planned on fucking and didn't say a word. Yet; you coming to me about Rhythm." It wasn't a damn thing she could say.

"Matter of fact, if I did pursue her or any other woman it's not a damn thing you can say about it."

"Kruz, really?"

"Really because you lost the privilege to question me on where I stick my dick."

"Son." My father finally spoke up. He knew just like my mom and Zahra, that I was about to go in.

"Nah pops. I'm tired of her tryna tell me who I can fuck, how I'm the one who made her cheat and whatever else she filling mom's heads up with. Zahra, hear me and hear me clear." I had my hand on the door because my anger was rising and I didn't wanna do something and later regret it. Especially; if she is pregnant with my baby.

"Your sister is best friends with her and to my knowledge, you hate her and the relationship they have." Her mouth dropped open.

"Yea, you of all people should know I do background checks on bitches I fuck with. Therefore; any and all information is told to me."

"Kruz, are you serious?" My mom questioned.

"Dead serious. Zahra, you have one time to confront Rhythm about anything and I'ma fuck you up."

"You don't even know her." I smirked because she had no idea.

"And neither do you. A woman being best friends with your sister doesn't exactly qualify as the person you grew up with." I shrugged my shoulders and stormed out the house.

"Girl, you better go after him." I heard my mom yell and my father dug in her ass. I hit the alarm on my truck and opened the door.

"So that's it Kruz? You leave me as a single mother and run to the next bitch with her legs opened?"

"Jealousy doesn't become you. And you had no need to be jealous when we were together because it was and had always been about you."

"I'm sorry Kruz. I just want us back together and..."

"Negative." I sat in my truck.

"You're already jealous over a woman who I haven't even gone out on a date with yet."

"A date? You're tryna make her your woman?"

"Who knows where it will lead me but you better not interfere with her or any woman you may see me with." I slammed my door in her face.

"As far as being a single mother, if that is my child you won't be raising him or her alone but you will be single because I won't be yo nigga. Don't get the definition of single mother confused." She rolled her eyes.

"Are you going to come with me to the doctors?" She wiped those fake ass tears.

"Text me the date and I'll go. If you text me about other shit, I'll block your ass." I lit the blunt, blew the smoke and pulled off. I'm over this bitch.

I watched my knight and shining armor pull off and broke down. Kruz's love for me was gone and it tore me apart listening to him speak on other women, especially; Rhythm. She may not have been my friend but it's a girl code. She knows I've been with him all these years and still had no problem pushing up on him.

Women throw themselves at Kruz so I know for a fact she did the same. I'm gonna make sure I do everything to make sure her or any other woman decides to mess with him. I'm not worried about him doing anything to me because I'm pregnant and his mom won't allow it. Plus, I'll be sneaky with it too.

I will be the bitter ex that people hate. The one to make a woman say, fuck this, all the drama ain't worth it. I'm telling you now so if this ain't a story you wanna keep reading, I suggest you stop because it's about to be on.

"You ok honey?" Mrs. Garcia hugged me and I cried harder in her arms. Yes, I'm upset about him not wanting to be with me, but I'ma milk the shit outta her.

"How can he cheat on me and not give me another chance for one mistake?" She started walking with me to my car.

"Don't you worry about a thing. We're going to work together and get him back to loving you." I turned and she smirked. I smiled and sat in my car.

"Are you sure?"

"Yup. Let's start off with him going to the doctors with you. Did you tell him when the next appointment is?"

"No. Let me text him now." I sent the message and told her I'd be by tomorrow. I stopped by everyday in hopes he'd show up and today was my lucky day.

I pulled off and headed to my mother's house to start some shit. Say what you want but the drama shall start today.

The Rhythm bitch is supposed to move in and help with the bills. Allegedly, my mother had trouble paying the mortgage. I would help her but no one told her to take equity out to fix the house up. It's been in our family for years and we were raised in it, however; it needed to be redone in which she did.

It definitely looks nice but my mom is an assistant manager at a nursing home. She doesn't make that much money so why she thought it was ok to upgrade is beyond me. I could've offered for her to live with me but then she'd have to bring my lazy ass sister and I'm not tryna argue in my own crib everyday.

Kalila graduated over a month ago and instead of making her get a better job, my mother told her to relax for the summer. She worked at the motel but that ain't no real job.

I didn't agree because she had been discussing not being able to afford the mortgage for months now. Why wouldn't she make her get a real job to help? It would definitely benefit the both of them. Now when I visit, this bitch will be there and so will Axel, who I love to death. I may hate his mother but he is my heart too. He can get whatever he wants from me.

I parked in the driveway of my mother's house and she came running out to ask me to move my car. When she asked me to move for the U-Haul my sister was on her way with, I took my keys out and placed them in my pocket. Those bitches can walk up the sidewalk with her shit. How much did she really have anyway? My mom had nice furniture due to the renovation and beds in the extra bedrooms. I could see anger on my mother's face and went past her in the house.

"TiTi Zahra." Axel ran straight to me. He wanted me to pick him up but I explained having a baby in my belly makes it hard. He waited for me to sit and hopped on my lap with his iPad.

"I miss you. Can we go to the mall and get the new Minecraft game?"

"Why didn't your mom get it?' I heard my mom suck her teeth.

"She says, it costs too much money. I can get it for Christmas. Do I have to wait?' I smiled and told him we could go later. He stayed on my lap until his mother and my sister walked in.

"MOVE THAT PIECE OF SHIT!" Kalila barked and I smiled. I knew she was mad because the 2018 Infiniti car I got is far from a piece of shit.

When Kruz took the truck away, I purchased a new car. I had an old Toyota Camry but I couldn't drive in that. Shit, he upgraded me a lot and I'll be damned if people assume I have nothing because we on a break.

"Not a chance. This baby has me tired and I need a nap." I rubbed my stomach and Rhythm shook her head.

"No wonder Kruz left you. Petty and childish ain't the word."

"Fuck you." Rhythm stepped out with Axel. She hated for anyone to curse around him and we tried not to but it happens sometimes.

"Nah, but I think Kruz would love fucking my best friend. You do know he finds her quite attractive."

"He's gonna use and abuse her like the rest of the bitches."

"Hmph. I don't think so."

"And why is that?" She smirked.

"Because he's already found out where she worked and asked her out. Most niggas tryna fuck, ain't tryna date." Her words stung because she was right. If Kruz was only fucking, he wouldn't have gone through all the trouble of finding a bitch.

"How are you ok with her fucking my ex. You're my sister and…"

"Stop right there." She put her hand up.

"You hate Rhythm due to your own insecurities, so don't you dare sit there and make it seem like she's stepping on your toes. And for your information she told Kruz she wasn't tryna deal with him because of you." I rolled my eyes.

"She may not have been your friend but she did tell him it's not ok to pursue her when he was with you."

"As least she has some respect."

"You just don't get it."

"Get what?" I was looking down on my phone waiting for Kruz to text me back. I sent a message before leaving his mothers about the doctor appointment and he has yet to respond.

"Rhythm may be telling him that, but he still asked her out. She isn't your friend so even if she does take him up on the offer, she's not wrong in no way. But you." She stepped closer to me.

"You hate that woman for no reason. A woman who fought battles with me for you." I didn't say anything because there were a few times bitches tried to step to me when I was with Kruz and they'd go find them and beat their ass. I never told him but I'm sure he knew.

"A woman who has decided to uproot her and my nephew to move in and help your mother out with the mortgage because your dirty ass refuses."

"She should've never upgraded. I told mommy to sell this piece of shit a long time ago."

"A piece of shit you can't stay out of. But don't worry, I'm getting a better job and making sure she doesn't ask you for a dime. Selfish ass bitch." She stormed out and I noticed my mother standing there wiping her tears.

"Ma, I told you before not to…"

"Just go Zahra."

"For what? I didn't do anything."

"You said enough and right now I don't want to look at you."

"FINE!" I snatched my things up and walked out the door with an attitude.

"Move this shit." I barked at the truck blocking me in.

"Nah. You can wait." Her and Rhythm started taking more totes out and placed them on the sidewalk.

"Axel wants me to get him a game." His head popped up. I am going to get it, just not today. Rhythm sucked her teeth and walked around the truck. She knew like I did, if you mentioned doing anything for Axel you had to do it. She hated to disappoint him.

"Fuck y'all." I shouted out the window and sped off. I don't need them or my mother.

****

"You're five months now. Do you want to know what you're having?" Kruz had his head in the phone grinning. I couldn't help but wonder who he was texting.

"KRUZ!"

98

"What B…" He caught himself and looked at the doctor.

"Ummm, I can tell you what you're having." She was nervous as hell.

"A'ight." He put the phone up and stood next to the machine.

"Looks like you'll need to purchase everything pink." I smiled while he had a frown on his face.

"You're not happy?" The doctor questioned.

"Hell no."

"Is it because you wanted a boy?" The doctor tried talking to him nicely but he was an ass.

"Nah because if this is my baby, I damn sure don't want a daughter. What if she grows up and be a ho like her mother?"

"Oh my." The doctor looked like she was about to pass out.

"Yea, this ho cheated on me. I don't even know if this is my kid." The fact he said it with no care in the world let me know how hurt he really is.

99

"Yo! Can we do the test where you can find out early if it's yours or not."

"You mean the amniocenteses?"

"Is that the one where you take blood or something and do a DNA test?"

"Yes."

"Yea. I need that done ASAP. I don't care about the cost."

"We can but mommy has to agree to it. Also, there are complications and…"

"Fuck all that. I don't care if she dies. I need to know if this is my kid before I buy a damn thing. Set it up Zahra."

"Kruz, you heard her say.-"

"And you heard what the fuck I said. Do it so I can tell any future women in my life about how petty and childish I know you're going to be if it is mine. Therefore; they'll have a choice to stick around." His demeanor was cold and hateful. At least he knew what would happen in the future.

"Let me give you two a minute." The doctor stood.

"We don't need one. Set it up." She looked at me and I nodded my head yes. She left the room and five minutes later returned with a time for tomorrow. I didn't know it could be done that fast but then again, he's paying cash so I'm sure she had no problem putting a rush on it.

"Have your ass at the hospital early."

"Kruz, wait!" I followed him out the doctor's office.

"Tha fuck you want?" He hit the alarm on his truck.

"Can we be cordial? I mean you're treating me like shit all the time." He gave me a crazy look.

"I messed up Kruz, but I'm still gonna have your child."

"Maybe." I grabbed his arm.

"I may have made a mistake but I used condoms."

"Condoms? Bitch, you said y'all fucked once. A mistake is one time." I didn't say anything.

"We don't need to dwell on the past." He sucked his teeth.

"Kruz, there's no doubt in my mind that this child is yours."

"Why now Zahra?" He leaned against the truck and I bit down on my lip. His man wasn't hard, yet; I could see him lying on his leg through the jeans, that's how well-endowed he is.

"Why now what?"

"You've been on the pill for years. I asked you for a kid last year and you claimed to wanna wait until you finished nursing school. Here we are a year later, you cheated and all of a sudden pregnant."

"When you asked me, I stopped taking them right away. It takes a while to get pregnant after being on the pill for years. I didn't tell you because I wanted to surprise you. I found out the morning I came to see you. I wanted you to make love to me and I planned on telling you in the middle of it." He didn't say a word.

"I can't apologize enough for making a mistake Kruz. If I could take it back, I would and I shouldn't have agreed for other women to please you orally. I messed up bad and you have no idea how bad I regret it."

"I'll see you tomorrow." He hopped in his truck and pulled off. His tone wasn't mean and I think he may give me another chance.

I walked to my car and picked up my phone that kept going off in my purse. The caller wasn't who I wanted it to be but I had to answer because he's a pain in the ass now. After Kruz left me, I stopped seeing him. This man doesn't seem to get the picture though.

"What?"

"Is that my kid?"

"Who told you I was pregnant and why would you assume it's your child?" I turned out the parking lot.

"You post on social media, remember? And we've had accidents."

"What?" I was confused and nervous at the same time. I watched him put condoms on each time. Was he taking them off? Then again, Kruz found one inside me so maybe more broke off in me than I realized.

"You weren't even gonna tell me, were you?"

"You were a mistake and…" He laughed in the phone.

103

"A mistake doesn't happen for a year. Now we got a situation because of the games you played."

"We don't have shit." I tried to sound tough.

"Stay in denial all you want. When the baby is born, I want a test." He disconnected the call. I pulled over and cried my eyes out. *What if this is his child?*

"Ok ladies, let's start from the top again." The dance instructor told us.

Kalila and I were taking twerk and pole dancing classes. Over the past few days, she started putting out tons of applications for a computer engineer but no one called back. Eventually, she started working more hours with me at the motel just to make more money.

We both made minimum wage, which is only $8.25 an hour. It wasn't enough to renovate the upstairs so we're taking these classes to strip a few nights a week. I know some may ask if she gave her mom all that money, why isn't it enough?

Evidently, her grandparents had taken a double mortgage out and the money she had been paying on, was for that. The equity and loans her mom took out to upgrade is what the 70 k paid for. Kalila said fuck it, they may as well finish the house and we put our names on a loan for 150k. The two of us purchased new cars and the rest went to the same people who did the downstairs.

105

The renovation upstairs started and all of us were staying in the living room and basement until its done. I didn't wanna keep uprooting my son but at least, we're altogether and getting things done. Axel could care less as long as he had the iPad. Zahra did get him the game he asked for to play on his PlayStation and that too kept him busy.

"There you go Rhythm. That's the way you do it ladies." I did an entire set to *Dance for you* by Beyoncé and he was the prop. I stood up and smirked at the hard on he had. It's no secret he had a crush on me. He was handsome and the way he could move his body had me fantasizing of how he'd do me.

"Your turn bitch."

"Well shit. I don't want you to get mad if I turn your man on." I flipped her the finger and all of us watched Kalila do her thing. I must say we were the shit.

"Ladies tomorrow night there will be a birthday party at this club in New York. The top ballers and even some celebrities will be there from what I hear. Who's down to use this as their first experience?" We looked at each other and smirked.

106

"We down." I said and a few other chicks said the same.

"If you can pull this off, a spot is yours at the club." He winked at me.

"What about the rest of us who don't wanna do it?"

"You can try the club out tonight because it's a probably gonna be packed. You can reserve a spot as well if you do good." She nodded.

"Now what I need to mention is, if you're unsure, do not and I mean do not show up. My name is on the line and I'll be damned if you fuck it up by freezing on stage." He's right. Dexter is known as one of the best dance instructors and has the best women on his team. I don't blame him for not tryna mess up his brand.

"Here is the time and place we'll meet." He handed everyone a card.

"If you don't have anything to wear, I suggest you hit up a lingerie store today and make sure the outfit is fire. Also, you will not remove all your clothes no matter what. The party is for a deacon and he doesn't know they invited strippers. You're providing the fantasy but not giving him too much."

"I'm cool with that." I took these classes to strip with strict rules on not showing my pussy. That will always be off limits.

"Any questions?" Everyone said no and started gathering their things.

"You ready?" Kalila asked and opened the door.

"Yes and no."

What you mean?"

"Yes because we can use the money. And no, because I don't really want any men touching me."

"Me either. Shit, we have to find some ballers." I gave her the side eye because Jamaica can definitely take care of her.

She's still refusing to speak to him. She wants him to work for her and I get it, however; he stopped trying after the first two weeks of her not responding. It's been two months and she's still having crying fits every now and then.

"Whatever. He's doing him." She shrugged her shoulders. I doubt she'd ask him anyway. Her mom has always instilled being independent growing up.

"Let's hit the mall."

"How much money you got?" I opened my wallet and pulled the money out.

"Two hundred. What about you?" She did the same and said $150.

"It's good enough to get some nice shoes and a cheap lingerie set from Vicki Secrets." Both of us smiled and headed to my car. I grabbed the paper off my windshield and read it.

Don't get too comfortable with yourself. Every stuck-up bitch has to be taken off her high horse at some point. I laughed and passed the note to Kalila. I'm sure its Zahra with her hating ass. If she only knew, Kruz and I haven't seen one another since the day at the motel.

He sent me a text a few days later saying he was fresh outta the relationship with her and didn't wanna drag me in with her drama. He also said, the test revealed the child is his and he's gonna do right by his kid. I understood but didn't really know what he meant. Were they a couple again? I had

no idea and didn't bother asking.

We still text to check up on each other every day but

nothing about hooking up or seeing one another ever comes up.

Its good though because I don't need her drama in my

life, nor do I wanna be a rebound chick. I'm feeling Dexter

anyway. We've gone out and he's nice. We kissed a few times

but sex isn't on my agenda right now. I haven't slept with a

man in three years because my baby father gave me gonorrhea,

so I'm good on sex for the moment. Of course I want it but I'd

rather do myself then be put at risk again.

****

"It's packed out there Kalila." We were peeking out the

side where the stage was. Men were everywhere and some

women sprinkled in.

"Say the word and we're outta here."

"You're not scared." I turned to her.

"Hell yea I am. Then I think about my mom and push

the fear to the back of my mind. I can't let her lose the house

Rhythm. My sister may not care but I do." I nodded, took her hand and went in the back.

"Here y'all. We're going to need it." Sabrina passed us two shot glasses and held up a bottle of Tito's. She's one of the chicks we met in class. The bitch is bad as hell and if I went that way, I'd do her.

"Is it a new bottle?" I asked. I've seen Players Club and ain't no bitch date raping me.

"Girl bye. You know I don't play that open bottle shit." She used her teeth to open it and poured each of us a shot.

"Another one." We had four shots a piece and a bitch was ready to go to pass out. I drink occasionally so these shots had my head spinning.

"Rhythm, you're up." Dexter said and came close.

"You're gonna be fine." He placed a kiss on my lips and smacked me on the ass.

"You good?" Kalila walked with me to the door. I stood on the side of the dance floor and nodded at the DJ.

"Coming to the stage is a newbie. I must say, I've seen her rehearse and when I say you're about to spend all your money on her, believe it. Ladies and gentlemen, I give you Lavender." I snickered at the name he called. I could've used my own but everyone said, strippers had a stage name and that's all I could come up with on short notice. The DJ smiled at me, and cut the lights. Once the beginning of the song played, the club lit up in lavender lights. Here I go.

One lover, don't you dare slow down.

Go longer, you can last more rounds,

push harder,

you're almost there now, so go lover.

Motivation played loud on the speakers as I made my way to the pole. I hopped on, climbed to the top and arch my back on the way down. I let my legs open in a split and spun around the pole. Once I hit the floor, I found myself crawling to the edge of the stage. I saw the man of the hour sitting in a chair smiling hard as hell.

I continued my dancing but when Kruz and I locked eyes, I winked and he came closer to the stage. He gave zero fucks about blocking the birthday guy and no one moved him out the way.

I let my hands run up his chest as I stood. My pussy was in his face and he had no problem with it. He bit down on his lip and ran his hands up and down my legs; sending shockwaves through my body.

I squatted and bounced my ass to the beat and stared in his eyes. The two of us were lost in one another and everyone knew it. I leaned back on my hands and lifted myself in a handstand position against the pole. My legs opened, and as I finished my set, Jamaica came into view. I got nervous because if he sees Kalila in here, it was gonna be a problem. Together or not, he ain't having that shit.

"DAMNNNN!" The DJ said when the music stopped.

"We have to take a short break so she can get her money off the ground and these niggas can jerk off in the bathroom or something." I took the bag out security's hand and started picking my money up.

"Come here." He yanked me in front of him after I made sure all of it was in the bag.

"I don't know what's going on and why you had to revert to stripping but ma, you did your thing." Kruz said holding me close.

"I'm glad you enjoyed it."

"I did and make it your last time." I backed away and looked in his eyes.

"Kruz, you're not my man. Remember, you're doing right by your daughter and…" He crashed his lips on mine and I melted.

"Excuse me! Why are you kissing on my girl?" I heard Dexter asking and became embarrassed.

"This yo man?" I looked from Dexter to Kruz and shook my head yes.

"End that shit tonight." He whispered in my ear, kissed my cheek and walked off.

"Rhythm, I had no clue you were messing with him."

"I don't Dexter. I mean we were gonna hook up but he went back to his ex." I glanced over at the bar and saw him staring at me as he leaned on it. I hated he was so cocky.

"You sure because I love my life."

114

"Dexter, I like you but I'm not sure what he has up his sleeve and I don't want you caught up either."

"It's all good. Let's go see how much you made." He held my hand in his and let it go when Kruz started in our direction.

"Get yo shit."

"Kruz, you don't get to tell me what to do." Dexter walked away without saying a word.

"Coming to the stage is Lavender's best friend and I have to say she's just as good. Get yo paper ready."

"FUCK! Kalila here too." I turned to see Jamaica standing in front of the stage with his arms folded.

"Oh my God! I didn't get a chance to tell her y'all were here." Drunk in love started playing and the second she walked out, shit hit the fan. Kruz snatched me up, handed me the keys to his truck and told me to wait outside for him.

"I can't leave Kalila."

"Go get her." I ran in the back, and grabbed the bag of money. She wasn't back there so I told Dexter and Sabrina to run because shit was crazy. Once I got outside, I saw Jamaica

throwing her in his ride. At least, I know she's safe.

I was standing at the bar with Kruz and a few other guys on our team, talking about starting more businesses up here. One of the people we grew up with became a deacon of the church and today was his birthday. Kruz and I asked the Dexter guy to send us some of his new strippers but only the ones who could really dance. He's known as the go to guy when it comes to stripper shows and anything else regarding dancing.

The first stripper out was named Lavender and all of us laughed at the name because who would make it their stage name? The lights were low and the color of her name. It was hard to see who she was in the beginning because she started her set on the pole. She did a damn good job too but the second her identity became visible, all of us turned our heads except Kruz.

I knew he was feeling Rhythm but cut her off so it wouldn't be any shit with Zahra. After seeing the way, the men lusted for her, he made his way to the front with all of us behind. We kept our backs turned as she performed for him. It

117

may have started with her doing it for the money but the way those two got lost in each other, we knew the remainder of her set was for him.

He took her off, moved to a corner and took his shirt off to cover her body and I didn't blame him. No man wants others to witness what they have or will. I'm no fool either and once I saw her, there wasn't a doubt in my mind Kalila was coming up. They're best friends and did everything together from what she told me, when we did talk.

I can't front. Over the last two months, I missed the fuck outta Kalila. I know she wanted me to work for her and in the first two weeks, I did. She got flowers, candy, stuffed animals and whatever else I could send her. It didn't make her call me so I gave up. I found myself working more and indulging in more sex just to occupy my time. I refused to stay at my crib without her because it didn't feel the same sleeping in an empty bed.

Now I'm standing in front of this stage waiting on her to come out. Drunk in love came on and the second she graced the stage, I snatched her the fuck up. Some of the men we didn't know started popping shit, gunshots rang out and chaos erupted. I grabbed Kalila, tossed her over my shoulder and walked out. Ain't no way in hell she was about to strip for anyone but me.

"Get off me Kenron." Her punches in my back did nothing. I put her in my truck and said if she got out, I'd put her in the back with the child locks. I saw Rhythm pulling out the parking lot and stopped her.

"Where's Kruz?"

"I don't know. He told me to get Kalila and leave. Shit!" She jumped out the car still wearing his t-shirt and ran in the club.

"RYHTHM!" Kalila shouted, jumped out and ran behind her. I was right behind them and saw niggas laid out on the ground.

"KRUZ! KRUZ WHERE ARE YOU!" Rhythm walked through the club with no care in the world. Her and Kalila stepped over dead bodies and kept calling Kruz.

"FUCK!" I found him against the wall wrapping a belt around his leg.

"Are you ok?" Rhythm dropped next to him and checked his body.

"I'm good."

"Nigga, you were out before me. How the hell you get hit?"

"I came back in to make sure this stupid bitch left." Rhythm seemed offended.

"Not you."

"What bitch?"

"Me." Zahra came waddling over with an EMT worker.

"What the hell?" Rhythm shouted.

"Bitch, why you in a club and you pregnant? What the hell is wrong with you?" Kalila started going in.

"EXACTLY!" Kruz said and the EMT helped him up and brought a stretcher in.

"Why are you in a club?" Kalila asked again and Zahra sucked her teeth.

"My man said he was going to a club so I followed to make sure he was safe."

"Last I checked, my boy don't need no fucking security." She pissed me off saying it.

"I didn't mean it like that Jamaica. I didn't want no bitches tryna push up on him." She stared straight at Rhythm.

"Man? You're a couple?" I was shocked myself because he ain't tell me that. And after he snatched shorty off the stage, I bet he was about to take her with him.

Kruz never got the chance to answer because they rushed him out. I know he wanted to answer but the pain on his face wasn't missed. He may be a big dude but a bullet still hurts.

"That's right. He's my man so you tryna put a show on for him ain't gonna make him leave me. Nice try though and sis, why are you stripping? It doesn't become you at all."

"BITCH!" I had to hold Kalila back. She was trying her hardest to get Zahra.

"Jamaica, I didn't know you were fucking my sister."

"Who said we were fucking?" She had the nerve to smirk.

"We should double date." She looked Rhythm up and down and scoffed up a laugh.

"Kruz wants his woman to be a queen at all times. You just proved you're ratchet and ghetto like the rest of these bitches out here." She shrugged her shoulders and now I had to hold Rhythm back.

"Let me go check on my man."

"I can't do this." Rhythm had a hurt look on her face.

"Tell Kruz, I hope he feels better but when he does to please leave me alone."

"He's not with her."

"It doesn't even matter. I refuse to deal with her bullshit over a man I haven't even been with. I'll keep my peace with Dexter." She looked at her friend.

"You coming?"

"Yea."

"Kalila, I'll be by to get you later." She waved me off. I wanted to go after her but I also needed to make sure my nigga was good. I hopped in my truck and waited for the girls to pull off.

When I arrived at the hospital Zahra's sneaky ass was smiling hard as hell in her phone. Its mighty funny how she claiming to be his woman and boo loving with someone else. It's all good though because when her shit comes to light, and it will, she better be ready for any repercussions that come along.

****

"Kenron, this isn't going to fix anything. Ssssss." I gripped Kalila's hips tighter and dove deeper in her pussy.

"Fuck baby. Yesssssss. I missed this." Her juices flowed right in my mouth. I kissed her thighs, then her stomach.

"I want you to have my baby." Her head popped up.

"I'm serious." I placed myself at her tunnel and stared in her eyes.

"I'm in love with you too K." She smiled and let the tears roll down the side of her face. I kissed each one away and thrusted inside her. A tingle went down my spine as we became one again.

It took her leaving me to realize how much I needed and wanted her in my life. Shit didn't seem right without her. Kalila was perfect for me in every way and like all men, I had to push my pride to the side and get outta my own way to see it.

She wrapped her legs around my waist and used her hands to push me in deeper. She slid her hands to my back and I felt her nails digging with each deep stroke I gave her.

I watched her gasp as another orgasm overtook her body. Instead of pulling out, I drilled deeper and deeper until she screamed out. When she shouted she couldn't cum anymore, I pumped harder and faster, stretching her pussy any and every way I could. She would definitely be walking funny tomorrow.

"I'm gonna cum again Kenron. Of fuck! Right there." Her body grinded under mine and she wet my dick up so much, I had to pull out in order not to cum myself. We've been apart for a minute and I needed to be in as long as possible.

"Get up here." I laid on my back and seated her directly on my dick. The pain showed in her expression but she took it like a champ.

"You gonna have my kid K?" I sat up and sucked on her breasts as she continued back riding me. Her hands were on my head.

"I can't hear you." I gave her a death stroke from the bottom and she cried out.

"Yes Kenron. Fuck yes. I'll give you whatever you want."

"You're my woman now." She nodded yes and I felt my nut coming up.

"I'm about to cum ma." She stood on her feet, rode me faster and I swear the amount of cum leaving my body better had gotten her pregnant.

"I love you so much Kenron." She had her head rested on my shoulder. I made her look at me.

"I love you too." She smiled.

"I had to stop denying how I really felt."

"Are you sure, you're ready to be with just me?"

"Serious as a heart attack. I missed the fuck outta you."

I squeezed her ass and kissed her deeply. I have no idea what this woman did to me, but I know no other man will have her. If I have to be monogamous to make sure it doesn't happen then so be it. She's more than worth it.

"Why were you stripping?" Kenron asked me this morning. We had sex all night and a bitch didn't wanna move at all.

"I don't wanna talk about it." He lifted my chin off his chest.

"Why were you stripping? If you needed money, all you had to do is ask." I smiled because he's always told me to ask if I needed anything. I blew my breath in the air and rolled on my back.

"My mom almost lost the house." He sat up and looked at me.

"The house has been in our family for years and my mother didn't wanna sell it. On top of the remaining balance of what my grandparents owed, she took out equity and another loan to upgrade the house. Baby, the house needed it really bad." He nodded.

"Anyway, she didn't wanna tell me to work more hours because of me finishing school. Long story short, she planned on letting the house go into foreclosure and we were gonna move into the projects." He turned his face up.

"Rhythm stepped up and moved in to help with the mortgage." Damn, my best friend definitely had our best interest at heart more than my own sister.

"I gave her all the money in my account and had her pay the rest of the mortgage off." I explained how all the money he gave me, I saved some and gave it to my mom. He said, he respected it and promised to refill my account with even more.

"Rhythm and I, then took out another loan to get new cars to get back and forth to work. We gave the rest to my mom to have the rest of the house done. Still it wasn't enough because we didn't wanna be paying off the loan forever, therefore; we decided strippers make a lotta money. Last night was our first night doing it in front of an audience; well hers anyway." I wiped the tears coming down my face.

"I couldn't let my mom lose the house Kenron."

"Come here." He sat me on top of him.

"Do you know my mother asked Zahra to help and she said no, it's not her problem my mom wanted to upgrade."

"What?"

"Yup. I know for a fact she could've helped because I've seen all the money in her account. Let alone, she's a damn nurse."

"How much is the loan you and Rhythm took out?"

"I don't want you to give me money Kenron. I'll figure out another way to pay it off."

"How much?"

"150 k." I whispered and put my head down.

"I can't hear you." I repeated myself and he asked which bank.

"Get dressed."

"Huh? I thought we were staying in for the day and my pussy hurts." He laughed and picked me up.

"Tell Rhythm to get dressed too." I told him I'd text her when we get out the shower. He didn't have to come out and tell me he's about to pay the loan. The least I could do is make it worth his while.

"Got damn K." I twirled my tongue around on his dick and continued suctioning my cheeks in and out.

"Stand up and turn around." He didn't let me finish.

"Why?"

"I'm about to nut and if you're gonna have my babies, I can't have you swallowing them." I laughed and gripped the railing in the shower when he forced his way in.

"Throw it back K. Yea, like that."

SMACK! He pumped a few more times and once I clapped my ass for him on it, he let go and didn't pull out until he went soft.

"You're the fucking best Kalila." He yanked me by the hair and kissed me aggressively.

I washed him up and both of us got dressed and left his house full satisfied. My pussy was sore as shit but it's worth it.

I smiled as he drove to my house. I had a man, possibly a baby and my mother will be happy as hell to know, none of us will have to something strange, for a piece of change.

****

130

"Where we going?" Rhythm jumped in the car and I noticed a hickey on her neck. I wanted to question where it came from but not with Kenron in the car.

"I see you had a good night." Kenron asked anyway.

"Please. Kruz did this when he pulled me off the stage." She waved us off and asked again where we were going.

"To the bank."

"The bank?"

"Kenron's idea."

"Oh, he must've thrown it on your ass if you calling him by his real name."

"Whatever bitch. I always call him both names, don't I baby?" He turned to look at me.

"You do, but I love hearing you say it when I'm digging in that banging ass pussy."

"Ok. TMI!" She shouted from the back and asked him to turn the radio up. We both laughed and kept stealing glances at one another the entire way.

"When we get in here, whatever you do Kalila, don't overreact ok." He squeezed my hand and opened the door before I had time to react.

"Hey baby."

"Baby?" I questioned in a whisper and Rhythm stared at me. The woman was Jamaican looking and pretty. Her body was ok and she dressed decent.

"I need to speak with your manager."

"Ummm ok." The chick said and couldn't keep her eyes off him. She walked away, into an office and came out with some guy.

"What's up Kenron? Ladies?"

"I need to make some transfers right quick."

"A'ight. Come inside."

"Kenron, we need to talk." The woman said and he ignored her. The guy closed the door and sat behind his desk.

"What can I help you with?"

"My girl and her friend took a loan out and I wanna pay it off." Rhythm tried to protest but he told her to be quiet.

"Ok. Let's see what we have here. Ladies, can I have your name?" We gave him our information and he had a weird look on his face.

"What?" Kenron became defensive.

"There's a loan out in Kalila and Rhythm's name for 150 k, but Rhythm did you come in and take out another one?" We both looked at her. If she did, I had no idea.

"Hell no!"

"I asked because someone used your information and took out a loan for 250k."

"SAY WHAT!" She jumped out her seat.

"How the hell is that even possible? Don't you need ID to take out a loan? I don't have that kind of money to pay the bank back. That's why we did a loan together." She started pacing the room.

"It wasn't done in this bank and yes the person is supposed to have ID. It says the loan was taking out a week ago and wow!"

"What?" She ran behind his desk and tears ran down her face.

"What the fuck is going on?"

"Someone purchased two Mercedes trucks under my name. A house is pending and there are three different credit cards in my name. My credit is going to be ruined. How am I going to prove that's not me? Oh my God! What if the IRS comes after me for it?" I looked at Kenron who was typing away on his phone.

"I don't have that kind of money sis. What about my son? I can't lose him if I go to jail. I'm just gonna run away with him." She ran out the office crying. By the time I got out there, she was gone.

"Pay off the loan between the two of them, put in a claim for fraud and fix this shit." The guy looked terrified.

"How the fuck someone came in and put all that shit in her name is crazy. Call me when its fixed." He nodded and we walked out to try and find Rhythm.

"Kenron what's going on?" I asked because this woman was now following us out the bank.

"Get in the car."

"Kenron, you better answer your wife right now!"

When she said that I dropped his hand.

"Tell me she's making that shit up."

"I'm not making anything up. He's my husband and I'm trying to figure out what he's doing with another woman."

"Get in the car Kalila." I did like he said because I had no ride.

I watched him walk over to the woman and start blacking out on her. I couldn't understand what he was saying because it was in another language but whatever it was, made her cry. He came to the car, slammed the door and sped off. He tried to hold my hand and I snatched it away.

"Kalila, not everything is what it seems." He said pulling in front of my mother's house. I saw Axel riding his bike with my mom watching.

Is she your wife?"

"Kalila."

"Is she your wife?"

"Yes."

"That's all the information I needed. Goodbye." I grabbed the door handle.

"Hold up. Aren't you gonna listen to what I have to say?"

"Once you verified her being your wife, there's no need." I opened the door.

"You know Kenron, you told me once, I'm the one you told all your secrets too. I guess you kept the biggest one to yourself." I slammed the door and ran inside. I went in the basement, plopped on the couch and cried like a baby. I just told this man I'd have his babies and he had a wife the whole time.

"When you're ready to hear me out, you know how to find me." I jumped at his voice.

"Oh, another thing." He came close and kneeled in front of me.

"If you even think about stripping, or doing other outrageous shit to make money, I promise to find you and cut your got damn throat." My eyes got big as hell

"Once you said yes to being my woman, there are no outs ma. Try some stupid shit and your mom will be setting up your funeral faster than you can ask me why." He pressed his lips on mine and walked out. What type of savage did I commit too? I thought Kruz was the only one. I guess birds of a feather really do flock together.

Mad wasn't the word for how I was feeling at the moment. Not only did my girl feel like she couldn't come to me for help, my fake ass wife thought it was a good idea to shout it out. Yea, she's my wife and I fuck her from time to time, but there's no feelings involved. Shit, we don't live in the same house, have any kids together or even go out in public. The only thing we share is a last name.

Kandy is the connects daughter we deal with and I only married her because her pops asked me too. He's from Guyana and had a green card, but his family were here on a VISA that was about to run out at the time.

His wife was safe because she lived in the US, where Kandy's mother and him were no longer together and he could care less about her being here. His son married a white woman and his other daughter married some guy from California. Kandy was the only one who needed someone to keep her around.

When we first started doing business with him, he explained how distraught he was about one of his daughters possibly being deported. My young ass saw a photo of her and she was beautiful. I was like ok, I can marry her, get my dick wet and go on about my business so I volunteered.

Her father sent us to the justice of peace and had it done ASAP. He purchased us a mansion and I had to show proof of us living together for at least five years. It didn't stop me from getting my own place and distancing myself from her. I knew after the stipulation time was up, I'd be doing me in public and its exactly what happened with K.

I met Kalila when she was a sophomore in college and we clicked instantly. It took me a few months to get the pussy and come to find out, it was because of her virgin status. Once I broke it, she became mine and mine only. I was very protective of her and what we shared.

I never told her about the marriage because in my eyes, she's not my wife. On paper yes, but not for real. Kruz told me not to do it because he felt eventually it would be a problem and after seven years, it hasn't been up until now.

Kandy thought her pussy would want me to stay married to her. Little did she know Kalila's is way better. The reason she did all that extra shit at the bank is because I served her ass with divorce papers two days ago and she's been tryna contact me ever since.

I couldn't move forward with Kalila knowing I'm married to her. I planned on telling her today but she mentioned the loan, gave me some banging ass head and sex in the shower; and I got sidetracked.

Now I'm back at Kandy's job waiting for her to come out. I told her I'd be back when I dropped my girl off and we're gonna have a talk. I said a few more things to her that made her cry and I didn't give a fuck. You don't get mad and shout shit out to be funny.

I made sure the divorce papers were still in the glove compartment because she's gonna sign them today, whether she wanted to or not. One thing I'm not gonna do is play games with her. Women tend to try and reconcile or even delay the process and I'm not having it. It's not like she'll be returned to her country because she's considered a citizen now. I stepped out my car when I saw her coming out the door.

"Kenron." I handed her a pen.

"What's this for?" She had a confused look on her face.

"We discussed that once our five-year anniversary hit, you would sign the divorce papers. Granted, I gave you an extra two years but your time is up."

"Kenron, I don't wanna divorce and…" I took my gun out and placed it under her chin.

"You don't have a choice, per the agreement you signed." I referenced the paperwork her father had drawn up before we got married. It stated once the five years hit, we can get a divorce and no one is to contest it regardless if the other party agrees or not.

"Kenron, I'm pregnant." I laughed at her.

"We both know it's not my child." I fucked her the other day and before that it had been a year.

"I didn't say it for that reason. I'm telling you because this is stressful and what if I lose the baby?"

"Sign the papers and you never have to see me again."

"Kenron please."

"Are you ok?" Some lady asked walking in our direction.

"I'll blow your fucking head off if you don't sign them before she gets over here." I cocked the gun. She cried and took the pen out my hand. She knew I didn't play games.

"This last spot here." She signed it and I checked to make sure it's her signature.

"I'm ok Rachel. We were talking about old times." She looked at me.

"Get your stupid ass outta here." The woman jumped and went back in the bank.

"I'm not gonna have any more problems outta you, right?" She nodded and I went to get in my car. I hit her with the peace sign and drove off. I thought about going to get Kalila but I'll give her a day or two for her pussy to heal before I beat it up again. Oh, hell yea, she's gonna regret not letting me explain.

****

"Why do I feel like Kandy is about to cause problems we don't need?" Kruz asked sitting up in the bed. He came home last week and hasn't really been outside. We aren't sure who shot him and he didn't wanna get caught slipping. He did at the club but then again, we had no idea anyone had beef with us or him.

"It ain't shit her pops can say. He's the one that had the agreement drawn up. He needs to be happy I gave her an extra two years."

"You don't think she'll come after Kalila?"

"I hope not because then we'll really have a problem. That reminds me, have you spoken to Rhythm?"

"Yea. I called to thank her for making sure I was good at the club and she started telling me what went down at the bank."

"That's some shit ain't it?" I shook my head in disbelief, still thinking about how someone was able to do that shit.

"Yea." He smirked.

"What the fuck you hiding?"

"Nothing."

"The hell you smirking for then? Don't tell me y'all fucked."

"Nah. I think she may be the one tho."

"Bro."

"I'm serious. The conversations we have are deep as hell and we've learned a lot about each other."

"Oh word?"

"Yea but I haven't told her about this bitch staying here until she delivers."

Ever since the results came back that Zahra is indeed having his kid, she's been complaining about being alone, having contractions and all this other shit. His mom told him, it's only right for him to be around in case she goes into labor. I couldn't believe his mom entertained the shit. We all knew she slept with the other dude more than once but the fact remains, it is his kid.

"You know she's not gonna be ok with it. Wait! How you supposed to spend time with her? She lives with Kalila and I told you all the shit going on."

"I'ma have to use my other house out in Sayreville."

"Damn. It's been forever since we been out there." We both had houses in different parts of New Jersey, one each in New York, Ohio, Kentucky, Texas, ATL, Phila and Maryland.

We got one in every state we did business in. And we'll be expanding soon to the West Coast.

"I know. I had a maid service go there the other day. The landscapers are always on point and I made sure the pool was cleaned out."

"Nigga, it's September."

"And it's still warm out. What if she wanna fuck in the pool?" I busted out laughing.

I stayed over there for a few hours with him in the office. We made sure employees were paid and business was running with no issues.

I checked my phone and saw another call from Mr. Euburne on my way out. I guess Kandy told him we're divorced. I answered just to get the conversation outta the way.

"What up?"

"Divorced now huh?" He laughed.

"Finally."

"I don't understand the issue tho. You gave her two extra years. If you don't mind me asking, what's the change?" I pulled in front of my house.

"I found someone and trust me when I say, she is not the type that's gonna let me stay married even if it is only on paper." He chuckled.

"I get it. Kandy's mother tried to get me to do what you did and Sunny wasn't having it." Now it was my turn to laugh. His wife is funny as hell and I always enjoyed going to their dinners.

"Listen son." I didn't mind him calling me that.

"The guy Kandy is allegedly pregnant by isn't happy after hearing about the marriage."

"What you mean?"

"Evidently, she hid it from him too. Luckily, she's pregnant and he didn't put his hands on her. However; he is seeking revenge on you."

"For?"

"Pulling a gun on her."

"You know I wouldn't hurt her but she wouldn't sign the papers." It was the truth. Kandy and I had an agreement and feelings weren't involved but I didn't want her dead. Me pulling the gun out was more or less to scare her. However; if it came down to it, I may have.

"I'm gonna send you his information. I refuse to have you out there blind." I opened the door and smiled.

"Send me that info. I'll call you when I get it." I didn't wait for a response and dropped my phone on the table.

"Do I have your attention?" K asked dressed in an outfit similar to the night I drug her out the strip club. I haven't seen her in a few days and I didn't stray. I knew she'd be back and let me explain. I must say, this introduction is the fucking bomb.

"Hell motherfucking yea." I licked my lips and walked closer to her.

"Damn." She pressed the button to my stereo and *Drunk in Love* came on.

"Why this song?"

"Two reasons." She moved me back and seductively danced in front of me.

"They are?" I kept putting my hands on her and she'd smack them away. I couldn't help it because she was so damn sexy.

"It's the only one I practiced my set to."

"And two?" She turned and gave me her full attention.

"It's how I feel about you Kenron." I smiled and let her finish performing. All I can say is afterwards, I tore her shit up. If she wasn't pregnant before, she is now.

"You need anything?" Zahra asked on my way out the door. She's been irking the fuck outta me. After the shooting, her and my mother thought it would be good for her to try and nurse me back to health. I, on the other hand wasn't beat. It's bad enough, I let my mom talk me into letting her stay sometimes when she felt alone until the baby came. I made her stay in one of the guest bedrooms down the hall and bring clothes over daily. She wasn't in any way moving back in my shit.

She's the reason I couldn't spend time with Rhythm like I wanted to and trust me, I did and it was before the strip show. However, once the results came back that the baby is mine, I figured why not try and do right and make sure her mom is ok throughout the pregnancy. Why in the hell did I do that?

The bitch tried countless times to give me a sponge bath, massage or even lie in my room to watch movies. Each time, I curved her and slammed the door in her face. I don't know why her ass isn't getting the picture. It's not like I woke up one night and went to her.

Shit, I had to get Kommon to come over and put a deadbolt lock on the door, just so she wouldn't try and pick the lock. Luckily, she wasn't there when he came because she'd probably beg him not to. He thought the shit was funny, where I wanted her the fuck out. Tryna be nice and listening to my mother, now I have a got damn stalker down the hall from me. I can't wait for her to deliver because she's getting the fuck out.

"Nah." I slammed the door behind me and limped to my car. Whoever shot me didn't do a good job. The bullet went in on the side and right back out. I'm only limping because there's still some pain. Not enough to keep me from my going to my destination.

"WHAT?" I barked in the phone.

"What if I go into labor Kruz?" This the shit I'm talking about. I literally just left and whatever she needed to say, could've been done in the house.

"Call my mother. I'm out." I hung up and blocked her ass.

I drove to my other house, pressed the code and left the gate open for my guest arriving shortly. I stepped out and admired the landscaping. I'm not here a lot but when I do come it's peaceful as shit. No one knows about this spot but Jamaica and now her. I could've taken her to a hotel but that's so impersonal and she deserves more than that.

When I called thanking her for checking up on me at the club, she started crying and telling me someone committed fraud in her name. I quickly paid for her and her son to stay in a hotel. She was scared and I couldn't scoop her up at the time. I was shocked she spoke to me after the BS Zahra pulled at the club.

I wanted to respond when my ex shouted I was her man but the EMT's rushed me out. Jamaica told me she was hurt and I understood. It didn't stop me from wanting her and vice versa. Today was gonna be the first day we saw one another in two weeks and a nigga couldn't wait.

I closed the door, took my bag upstairs and hopped in the shower. I started to take one at home but then Zahra would ask who I'm getting dressed for and I didn't wanna argue. If I could've left this morning I would have.

However, my mother came over tryna get me to take my ex back and discussing all the things she wanted to do with her granddaughter. She was doing too much too and the minute we had time alone, I'm gonna make sure she knows.

"I'm here." She spoke in the phone when I answered. I looked on the cameras and watched her pull in. I pressed the button to close the gates and went to open the door. She glanced around when she stepped out her car.

"This is very nice Kruz. I thought you lived by me."

"It's a long story and tonight is all about you." I took her hand in mine and turned her in a circle.

"You wore these leggings on purpose."

"Maybe." She stepped past me and brushed her ass against my dick.

"Stop playing."

"Who said I'm playing?" I locked the door and followed her as she toured the place on her own. She stopped in the kitchen and stared in the backyard.

"Axel would love a place like this." I wrapped my arm around her waist and placed my chin on top of her head.

"A pool, basketball court and humongous yard all in one spot. A kid would get lost." I turned her around, cupped her chin, tilted her head back until our eyes met.

"You're beautiful Rhythm and your heart is pure. If you were my woman, you'd have all this and so much more." I lifted her on the edge of the counter, opened her legs and stood in between.

"You seem perfect in a rude way but I'm not sure we'd mesh together."

"And why not?" I laid her back on the counter and removed her sneakers and socks.

"For one, you have baggage and... Sssssss." She slightly moaned out when I stuck her toes in my mouth. One by one, I sucked and watched her damn near cum.

"I've never had my toes sucked before. Shit, it feels good." I had a grin on my face listening to her say those words. I'm hoping to do a lotta first things with her.

"Lift up ma." My hands pulled down the leggings along with the thin see through panties.

"I'ma eat this juicy pussy and I want you to cum in my mouth when you lose control." I spread her legs opened and noticed wetness beginning to seep out. My finger stroked her mound a few times and just as it poked out, I latched on.

"Oh fuck!" She arched her back and placed her hands on her face.

Rhythm lifted her hips to meet my tongue and I lapped up all the nectar leaving her body. I let one of my fingers slip inside and her pussy clamped down. She was tight as fuck and I couldn't wait to be inside. How the hell am I gonna be able to fuck if she's this tight? I thrusted my finger deeper and listened to the moans.

"Stop holding it in Rhythm. Let it go." I sucked on her protruding clit and felt the wave flowing, along with more juices. Shorty was cumming hard as hell too.

"We not done ma." I took my clothes off and slid her closer to the edge.

"It's been a few years Kruz. Take it easy on me." I smiled. No wonder she's super tight.

"I got you." I grip the bottom of her cheeks, spread then open and slide her down.

"FUCKKKKK!" She dug her nails in my shoulder.

"You good?" Her face contorted with pleasure as I continued going in and out.

"Yessss. Don't stop." She wrapped her arms around my neck and kissed me in a way I've never been kissed. I can't even describe the feeling but I know I've never had it with anyone.

"Fuck me back." She nodded her head, had me sit and rode the hell outta me. When she turned around cowgirl style and did it, I was gone. My eyes were rolling, toes were curling and everything. Nothing prepared me for her jumping off and sucking every bit of cum I had out. It didn't help she was nasty with it.

"You good?" Now it was her turn to ask me.

"Yea. But we ain't finished."

"Oh no." She took my hand and led me out to the pool. I told my boy she'd wanna fuck in here.

We stepped in the water and she started giving me head on the steps. Our eyes connected and I knew then, she's the one. A woman with banging ass pussy and gives me head. Yea, I'll keep her.

"Turn around." I had her get on the edge, on all fours.

"What you about to do?" She asked over her shoulders. I smacked her ass and dove right in. My tongue took turns in her pussy and ass. She tried running but my arms held her there. After making her cum again, I brought her in the pool, lifted one of her legs up and forced myself in.

"Damn this some good pussy." The water was splashing everywhere as I slammed into her from behind even harder. I grabbed and held her hands to keep her from running.

"Kruz. Oh shit Kruz." Her pussy tightened up around my dick.

I spread her legs wider with my knee, pushing myself in deeper. My balls were smacking against her pussy with each thrust. The urge for me to cum is right there. I need to pull out but I can't because the feeling is so got damn good.

"Oh my God Kruz. I'm cumming again. Oh Goddddd!!!" She shook violently at the same time I let go of every seed in my body. I dropped her hands and placed my chest on her back.

"Shit! That was good." I fell on the steps and pulled her with me.

"I'm willing to give this, give us a try if you want." She turned and straddled me.

"You have a new baby on the way and..." I shushed her with my lips.

"I'm not a cheater Rhythm." She smiled and kissed me.

"You better not be." I felt her lower half grinding on me.

"I'm glad to see you're comfortable with my size."

"Oh, I'm sore but the pain is worth the pleasure I'm receiving."

"Good because I can stay in you all night." She stood, grabbed my growing dick and placed it inside.

"Then keep him there." The two of us had sex again outside, ordered takeout for dinner and christened almost every room in the house. I ain't tryna let her go. I just have to figure out a way to tell her about Zahra staying with me.

****

"Mmmm, baby this taste really good. You should try it." Rhythm tried to get me to eat shrimp scampi and I wasn't tryna hear it. I don't eat seafood at all.

"I like watching you eat it." I licked my lips reminiscing about the way we sex one another down. It's been two weeks since our first encounter and I must say, we more than satisfy one another.

After the first day we were together it's like we became joined at the hip. I'd leave to do some stuff and she'd go to work and spend time with her son, only to meet right back up with me. Kalila's mom didn't want him coming out late so she kept him for her.

158

I don't think she's mentioned to anyone besides her best friend that I'm the one she's been with. I only know that because her and Jamaica have been to the house a few times.

"What else you like watching me do?" She stuck her finger in her mouth and sucked the juices off.

"You stay playing games." She leaned over the table and pecked my lips.

"I'll play with him all day if you let me." Rhythm had a slick ass mouth but she always backed it up with some banging ass sex. You would think we knew each other longer because we held nothing back in the bedroom.

"Here's your check sir." The waitress passed me the black folder thing they put it in.

"I didn't ask for it." Rhythm had a confused look on her face too.

"No but she did." I saw my mother and one of her friends coming in our direction.

"Who is that?"

"My mom. Do me a favor Rhythm and try not to let anything she says get to you."

"What she about to say?"

"Who knows but she's team Zahra."

"Figures." She made a face and tossed her napkin on the plate.

"I promise to do bad things to you in the bedroom if you try and stay calm." She busted out laughing. I got that saying off the True Blood song she had me binge watching with her crazy ass.

"Hello. I'm Mrs. Garcia and you are?"

"I'm Rhythm. It's nice to meet you." My mom must've remembered the name because she sent her friend to their table. She never wanted people to know her shady side and trust; she has one.

"Well Rhythm, why are you with my son?" She said it in a nasty tone.

"Ma, what you want? Pops know you here about to act up for nothing?"

"Boy, I'm grown."

"Exactly and so am I."

"I just wanted Rhythm to know that your girlfriend is about to deliver shortly and she'll be non-existent. I don't want her to get attached."

"No disrespect Mrs. Garcia, but don't come over here trying to discuss his personal business. Not only is it rude but quite unnerving to see a woman of your age meddling in her sons' affairs."

"Excuse me!" I smirked when Rhythm stood.

"I'm aware of Zahra and I'm sure you're aware of who I am, since you're in cahoots with her. Let me be clear tho and feel free to run back and relay this message to her as well." I made my way in between because my mom will swing off and Rhythm might too.

"Kruz and I are two friends out having a nice dinner. I'm not tryna marry him or push out babies. However; I will continue to enjoy every second we're together because it's what I'm supposed to do. If this progresses into something more then, and only then will we have this motherly talk."

"Who do you think you're talking to?"

"Let's go ma. She wasn't rude or disrespectful."

"Goodbye Mrs. Garcia. I promise to send him home satisfied tonight so he doesn't take it out on her." When she blew my mother a kiss, I knew it would be a problem. She put my mother in her place in a nice way and I respected it. Inside I was cracking up.

"Kruz how are you going to let her speak to me that way?" I walked her outside to calm down.

"Ma, listen." I took in my surroundings to make sure no one was listening.

"I'm a grown ass man and who I'm out with is my business. Now I get you're team Zahra because we've been together for some years and you've grown to love her the same as I. But you're not the one she cheated on. The one she laid up next to after sleeping with another man. The one she went away with, when I assumed she was working. Or the one she sent out to get oral pleasure by other women."

"Son." I could tell she felt bad.

"Nah ma. I shouldn't have allowed women to do it but she set the stage."

"Huh?"

162

"We went out one night, I got drunk and she paid some stripper to go down on me. Ma, I didn't know until the next day because I thought it was her. I apologized because it was wrong and thought she would leave me. Do you know she told me, it's ok? I stopped speaking to her for days because I felt she didn't cherish our relationship." I was aggravated as hell because certain things should be private in your relationship but as usual, Zahra tries to make herself the good guy.

"I didn't know."

"I haven't stepped out as much as she's making it seem because I was still in love with her. But what I don't need right now is you tryna destroy any happiness coming my way."

"You don't have to worry about it Kruz." I turned to see Rhythm standing there visibly upset.

"What's wrong?"

"Nothing. I just wanna go."

"Son we'll speak later." My mother went in the restaurant and so did I to pay the tab. I came back out and Rhythm was gone. I walked to the truck and she wasn't there either. I didn't even have the energy to look for her. If she

wants me, she'll call.

I watched Kruz walk out with his mom and decided to get in on the conversation. I wasn't gonna be rude but my smart ass had more to say. Unfortunately, after coming up on their discussion I could hear the hurt and pain in his voice. Was he still in love with her? What if his mom is right about him showing me less attention when the baby arrives? Is he using me as a rebound chick to get over her? Sadly, I gave myself a headache thinking about it.

I could hear the sincerity in his voice when he asked what's wrong? His mother didn't smirk or say anything smart. The revelation he told her was as shocking to her, as it was to me. I knew their breakup was bad and she cheated but his feelings were still there. Four years is a long time to get over someone, and it will be harder adding a baby in the equation. Did I really wanna be bothered? As much as I didn't want to say goodbye, it's the right thing to do. He's not fully healed and I don't wanna get hurt.

The Uber pulled in front of the house and I hoped he'd come for me but when he didn't I knew he probably figured out why I bounced. I opened the door and saw Axel lying on the couch with his favorite nanny. This woman is Godsend and it's sad her biological child is sheisty.

I don't care what anyone says, she's been cheating and I bet it's with someone he knows. The bitch doesn't go anywhere so it has to be someone in this area and he knows everyone.

"Mommy." Axel ran and almost knocked me over.

"I didn't expect to see you until later or tomorrow." She smiled and put the remote down.

"What's wrong?"

"Axel can you give me and nanny a few minutes to talk?"

"Ok but can we play Minecraft when you're done?"

"Absolutely." He kissed my cheek and ran down the steps. I rested my head on the back of the couch.

"He still loves her."

"Who Zahra?" She laughed.

"Honey, I don't know what happened today but I can bet my life he doesn't wanna be with her." I turned my head to look at her.

"Does he have feelings for her? Probably and always will due to the time they have in."

"You didn't hear how he spoke about her." She asked what went down and I explained everything.

"First off... never let another woman or what you assume he meant or feels, run you away."

"But I..." she cut me off.

"Whether his mom felt bad after hearing it, she still got her wish and that was you leaving him. You should've let him explain and went from there. Look at me." She turned my face to hers.

"Zahra is my child but she's not the woman for him. I'm not saying you are either because it's new right now. But I saw the sparkle in your eye when mentioning him. You have a glow around you and you're happy. Rhythm it's been a long time and you of all people deserve it."

"What happens when she has the baby?"

"They'll co-parent. Sweetie, you met at an awkward time but if he's making you smile and it feels right, then fight for him."

"I can't compete with a newborn or any child."

"Then don't. When he's spending time with the baby don't assume it's more than what it is. If you want to be with him and for it work, trust and communication is the key."

"Mommy come on." Axel yelled from the basement. They were still renovating. I couldn't wait until they were finished.

"Thanks for the talk."

"Always." I took my ass downstairs to play Minecraft before Axel killed me.

****

"Bitch how about Zahra called me this morning asking why you were out eating with Kruz." Kalila busted out laughing. She's been to the house with me and Kruz a few times.

"What you say?"

168

"I laughed and told her stupid ass to get off my line." I shook my head.

"Why does she think he's outta town on business though?"

"What you mean?" I walked with her to the next room to clean. I kept my eye on the office in case anyone wanted to rent a room. We were working until four because the manager was coming in to work. He did his own audit once a month just to be sure the IRS couldn't take shit from him.

"If y'all together, why he telling her he's out on business calls? I mean he doesn't have to mention you but still."

"I don't know and at this point, I don't care." She turned to look at me.

"You fucked around and fell for him already." I used my two index fingers to catch the tears falling from my eyes.

I wouldn't say I'm in love with him but my feelings are way past lust and like. The late-night phone calls, deep conversations and amazing sex did it. And let's not forget, I haven't been with a man in three years. I guess the attention he gave, made me feel special. I missed being with a man so much, I fell for the first one who gave me the time of day.

"Does he feel the same?"

"I don't know and before you ask, NO! I'm not telling him."

"In this situation I wouldn't tell you to, however; I'd try and find out. Matter of fact, Jamaica told me he's really into you. I can have him pry if you want." She shrugged her shoulders and slid the key in the room we were about to clean.

"THA FUCK YOU DOING YO?" We turned around and there were two big guys standing there. The black van we constantly see was behind them and two other guys stepped out.

"Ummm, there wasn't a do not disturb sign on the door, so I went to clean it."

"Bitch, you don't see the fucking sign right here?"

"BITCH?" Both of us questioned and put our hands on our hips. The other guys walked in.

"You heard me. Stop running your got damn mouth and you would've saw it."

"Nigga you got us fucked up."

"Ain't nobody got shit fucked up but you. Do I need to tell the manager your violating the privacy policy?" Both of us stayed quiet because we needed this job. Jamaica may have paid the loan off but neither of us wanted to lose our jobs.

"That's what I thought. Stupid ass bitches."

BOOM! He slammed the door in our face.

"No the fuck he didn't." I went to knock and Kalila pulled me away.

"Girl they hiding something in there." We moved on to the next room and made sure it wasn't a sign on it.

"Why you say that?" I glanced over at the office and noticed a car pulling in.

"They stopped us from going in the room and notice how they blocked the door. You can't say the black van isn't suspicious."

"We'll discuss this when I come back."

"Where you going?"

"Someone just came." I pointed to the car.

"I'm coming."

"Kalila you have to clean."

"Girl you are not leaving me with those crazy men a few rooms down." We walked down to the office and stopped in our tracks. The man getting out the car was fucking gorgeous. He definitely had some Spanish in him, his body had a nice build and the suit he wore appeared to be expensive and that's because I'm going off the gold cuff links.

"Bitch, why he look like?" I cut her off.

"Can I help you?" He licked his lips and smiled.

"I'm looking for a woman named Rhythm Mitchell."

"Why are you looking for her?"

"If I told you why, then I'd be violating the code of my company. Do you know where I can find her?"

"She's not in. Leave your information and I'll make sure she gets it." He handed me a card and walked back to his brand-new Audi truck.

"Who the hell is that?" Kalila took the card out my hand.

"Kommon G. Insurance salesmen."

"You tryna buy insurance?"

"No." I snatched the card out her hand.

"It says health, life and all insurances available. The bank guy did contact me and say someone would be looking into what happened."

"An insurance guy tho?"

"Maybe it's insurance through the bank. Like fraud or something."

"I guess."

"Where you going?" I put the card on the desk.

"To finish cleaning. You helping?"

"Until someone comes." I followed her and the two of us cleaned and cut up. We ended up finishing early. I ordered lunch and we were out at four.

"I'm going to bed." I told her after getting home. We went food shopping after work, picked Axel up from after care, made dinner and crashed on the couch. I didn't expect her to be here this long because she's been staying with Jamaica.

"A'ight." Axel and I went downstairs, took showers and were knocked out by 8:30.

"What's so important you needed me to come here?" I asked my boy Ramon, who I been friends with since college. We weren't besties or anything like that, but still close.

"I don't have a lot of time to talk because my manager is having a fit about this." He closed the door to his office and offered me a seat.

"Ok. So what's up?" He turned the computer to me and I had no idea what it was until he told me it's some woman's information.

"Why you showing me somebody loans?"

"That's just it. They're not hers."

"I'm confused." He began explaining how my brother's best friend came in with two women to pay off a loan for his girl. I have to admit, I was shocked to hear Jamaica had, or should I say claiming a woman. His ass fucks more bitches than these celebrity niggas.

Ramon went on to say, the other chick is the best friend and someone opened up massive credit in her name from another bank. It's pretty fucked up because whoever did it, put

174

a house and other shit on it. If you know like I do, whoever's responsible is about to get fired.

The reason he's upset and worried is because he's a manager and a red flag should've come up on all their computers, especially; when those amounts of loans are taken out. However, the person did it or should I say whoever worked at the bank, opened them all in one day, which makes it worse. I don't know shit about banks so I have no idea why he even contacted me.

"Ramon, I hear all you saying but it makes no sense on why you contacted me. I do insurance."

"I know. Can you open up a fraud case and try to figure out who did it?"

"Don't y'all have people for that?"

"Yup but for some reason they're not putting a rush on it and I'm not tryna get fired. I been here ten years and worked my ass off to her in this position. I'll be damned if some idiot gets me fired for doing dumb shit. Plus, I don't feel like dealing with your brother or his friend."

"Come again." I lifted my head from texting this bitch I've been fucking. Her pussy fire but she on some other shit lately.

"Kenron told me I better fix it or him and Kruz would return." I sucked my teeth. I hated when they threw their weight around.

If you don't know, I'm the older brother to Kruz; Kommon Garcia. We aren't twins but get mistaken for it often. I'm not sure why, when he's darker and has more of a build. I'm not skinny and don't stay in the gym, but my body is decent. He has gray eyes and mine are hazel. If people can't distinguish we're not twins, it's their problem.

Anyway, it's no secret my brother and his friend have this state and probably others on lockdown. People are petrified of them and bitches wanna be on their arm no matter what the cost. It's crazy because even the cops know the shit they do, yet allow them to walk the streets. I guess when you have crooked law enforcement on your team, you become invincible.

I loved both of my brother's to death, even though the young one can't stop stealing for shit. My mother doesn't make it better by enabling him. I say enabling because he'll get caught and she laughs it off. I can't even tell you how many of my aunts, cousins and some uncles beat his ass for it. My pops says it's exactly what he gets, where my mom will get into arguments with them. To be honest, the only person Kash is scared of, is my father and Kruz.

"A'ight. Give me her information." I waited for Ramon to print it out and told him I'd talk to her. Whoever she is must have beef with someone if they opening credit in her name. I'll run her name through the database my company uses.

I'm an insurance salesman and no I'm not crooked. The reason I travel as much is because the clients I deal with are rich as fuck and most are considered high risk. Therefore; I'm the one who has to travel and make sure we can insure them. It's a hard job because some of them need million dollar polices but the company won't offer it unless I give them the ok.

A few cases I couldn't because these motherfuckers were jumping off the Grand Canyon and shit like that. Another case was a woman who sniffed coke like it was a job. I mean the bitch shouldn't even have nostrils, as much as she smoked. One guy swam with the sharks for a living doing research and shit. I could go on but you get where I'm going with it.

I didn't deal with fraud but Ramon knew my company did background checks on clients and they do look into everything. I'm not sure the bank will be able to do anything with the info if I did find out something, since it's not coming from their department but I'll still look for him.

I drove over to the motel listed as her place of employment and stepped out. For this not to be a hotel, it was in pretty decent shape. Most motels looked run down and had fiends and bad ass kids running through the parking lot. This one looked nothing like it.

Two women walked up on me and asked who I was. Both of them were pretty and had I not been in a rush, I'd probably kick it to at least one. The lighter one took the card and said she let Rhythm know I stopped by. For some reason it felt like she's her but again, I didn't have time to chit chat and find out if she is. I pulled off and answered my phone.

"Yo! Why you calling me nonstop?" I barked at this chick I used to fuck with. The pussy good and so is her head game but she played too many games.

"I miss you baby."

"Yea right."

"I do. Can I come see you?"

"For what? We ain't fucking." I would never stick my dick in her again even if she stood in front of me butt ass naked.

"Kommon, it's not all about sex but if you want me to suck you off I will."

"Nah. I'm good."

"Why do I feel like I'm losing you?"

"Bitch because you are or should I say did?" I was getting ready to hang up on her

"Bitch?"

"You heard me. This entire time you never mentioned having a man. I'm thinking it's about you and me, and later on find out it's the opposite. How the fuck you think that's ok?"

She stayed quiet on the phone.

"You put me in a position to come clean about something that would've never happened had you been honest. Do you know how this shit is gonna play out?"

"I'm sorry."

"Sorry ain't gonna fix anything when it comes out." I finally disconnected the call and drove to my mom's.

I parked and stepped out to see my pops sitting on the porch drinking a beer. He loved the outdoors and said it's his peace from my mom who can be overbearing and a pain. I took a seat next to him and rested my head on the back.

"How are you gonna fix it?" He asked without even knowing the problem. I swear between him and Kruz, they must have that sixth sense shit going on because they'll know stuff before you even say it.

"What would you do if you did something and had no idea there was a backstory behind it?"

"Is this pertaining to a chick?"

"Yup." I kept my head back and eyes closed.

"Is it bad?"

"You have no idea."

"Will the news hurt the person?"

"Without a doubt."

"If you know it's wrong, then it's better to get it out now because if not, it'll blow up and make the situation worse." I lifted my head and looked at him.

"Pops, I swear I didn't know until it was too late and I broke it off. The only thing is, she's not listening and constantly calling and asking me to come over and other shit."

I wasn't lying to my father. In my job, I travel a lot and barely make it home to visit. It's not that I didn't want to, it's my mother is too much and we don't really vibe with one another. Shit, I can't even tell you how many times she's been to my house because I couldn't be bothered. I love her to death but I'd rather deal with her from a distance.

What I do know is it's probably better to keep this shit to myself but then again, it may not be possible. My ass ain't no fighter and this secret is definitely gonna cause one. I kicked it with my father a little longer and went home.

Unfortunately, this bitch sat in her car at the end of my driveway. I kept going and stayed at a hotel. She just don't get it.

****

"Damn girl, you sexy as hell." I told the new chick I mess with. We've been messing around for over a month. We met at the club when Dexter had her perform with the other new girls he had. I asked her out on a date and we've been around each other ever since.

"You're sexy too." She sat across from me blushing like a school girl.

"I suggest you show me."

"I'm all about spontaneous sex but I'm sure we'll get an indecent exposure ticket in this upscale restaurant."

"I'll pay it if I can see your sexy ass riding me." She bit down on her lip and lifted her hand to ask the waitress for the check.

The thing I liked about this woman is she wanted this relationship to be 50/50. If I paid for dinner, she'd pay for lunch the next day. She wanted to make sure I knew she didn't need me or my money. Like most men, I appreciated it but it's my job to spoil a woman. Slowly, she's allowing me to do it.

"This is how we doing it?" I heard and rolled my eyes.

"Lets' go Sabrina." I stood, took $100 bill out my pocket to place on the table, grabbed my girl's hand and headed for the door.

"KOMMON GARCIA!" The bitch shouted my name out.

"Go to the car." I kissed Sabrina on the lips and gave her the keys. When she sat down, I turned and went in on this ho.

"Why the fuck are you following me bitch?" She instantly started crying.

"Your fucking tears don't move me. I do know if you keep popping up where I'm at, I'll let my brother know there's a stalker I need for him to get rid of."

"Kommon, I thought we were going to be together."

"That's before I found out you were dealing with someone close to me."

"Y'all don't even speak like that."

"SO THE FUCK WHAT. IT DOESN'T MEAN." I had to calm myself down because people were walking by staring.

"Stay the fuck away from me." I left her standing there crying and hopped in the car. Sabrina stared at me.

"What?" I snapped and didn't mean to.

"I don't wanna get in your business because whatever you had with her was before me but isn't that..." I cut her off.

"Yes and I didn't know."

"You need to tell him before she does because it's no telling what she's gonna say."

"I know." She placed her hand in mine and kissed the top of it. I swear this woman was slowly making me fall for her. I thought about dropping her off at home but asked her to stay with me. I needed to get some frustration out and she knows how to do it best.

"What the fuck you mean some bitches almost walked in the room?" I barked at one of the clean-up crew guys.

"Boss, we were pulling up to take the bodies out and..." I stopped him when my phone rang.

"Yea ma." I stepped out the conference room and shut the door.

"Your brother got arrested."

"Which one?" I asked because both of them do stupid shit.

"Kash."

"What the fuck he do?"

"The school called and said he stole two hundred dollars out the PTO box."

"How the hell he do that? Wait! Why is the money laying around?"

"I think they're lying son. Kash don't need to steal." I laughed hard as hell in the phone.

"Are you serious?"

"Yes I am. What's so funny?" I can picture my mom having her hands on her hips.

"You know damn well Kash is hella thief. That nigga steals from you. Hell, you told me last week he sold your laptop for money."

"That's different."

"Bye ma."

"Kruz are you going to get him?"

"Hell no. Let his ass sit there and think about the shit he did."

"KRUZ!"

"Why can't you or pops get him?"

"I'm helping Zahra set up the baby room and your father is working. I don't wanna bother him."

"Yea right. You know pops gonna beat his ass. And you better be fixing the baby room at her house because once she delivers, her ass is going home."

"You would throw your child's mother out to be homeless?"

"She has a place ma. Stop this shit with her."

"She gave the place up and go get your brother." The phone disconnected. I went back in the room and stared at these stupid motherfuckers.

"When there's a body in the room it should always be someone there until it's cleaned up."

"We went to..."

"I DON'T GIVE A FUCK!" I rubbed my temples and opened the door for them to leave. This is the only way I could calm down.

"I pay the manager good money to keep the room unavailable. It's convenient and no one really goes there. Don't make me kill you because y'all wanted to have lunch dates and shit. Tha fuck out my face."

PHEW! PHEW! I dropped two of them right before they hit the door. The other two were nervous as shit.

"Two dead because it was two women who saw y'all. Two women who could possibly identify your stupid ass if it came down to it."

"But they didn't see the guys in the room." I ran up on the one speaking.

"It doesn't matter. What if they hear about someone dying or missing and put two and two together?"

WHAP! I knocked the shit outta him with the butt of my gun.

"The shit was sloppy as fuck. Let it happen again and not only are the two of you next, so is someone in your family. Now get these dead motherfuckers out my got damn office."

"You good?" Jamaica asked.

"Take this ride with me." I walked over the bodies, down the steps and hopped in the truck. This day was already turning to shit.

"What?" I answered my phone without looking.

"Hey. You can call me later." I smiled hearing her voice. After the way she left a few days ago I gave her space.

"Nah, you good. What's up?"

"I'm hungry and I don't have a dinner date." Jamaica sucked his teeth. He hated when we spoke on the phone or in person. We were definitely all over one another.

"I can't help if you're gonna run off again."

"I'm sorry. I didn't appreciate your mom tryna come for me. Then I heard you speaking to her. I was in my feelings a little but I miss you."

"I miss you too. Where you wanna eat at?"

"You pick because clearly you hate seafood." I had to snicker because she tried to get me to eat it.

"I'll pick you up around 6 or do you wanna meet me?"

"You can pick me up because it's more room in there to make up. I wanna..."

"Hold up Rhythm. Jamaica in the truck and he can hear you."

"My bad. Hey Jamaica."

"What up?"

"I'll see you later Kruz." I told her the same and hung up.

"Don't you say shit." He put his hands up.

"All I'm gonna say is make sure your feelings are real and not rebound ones."

"Why you say that?"

"It's obvious she's in love."

"Not yet."

"Trust me. She is." I smiled on the inside. My feelings were definitely involved but he's right. I need to make sure they're genuine and not replacing Zahra.

****

"Ouch!" Kash yelled out when I punched him in the chest. I could see him tryna catch his breath.

"Tha fuck you stealing from the PTO for?"

"Bro, they had the money on the table in the lunch room unattended. Why would they leave it, if they didn't want somebody to take it?" I looked at Jamaica and we both busted out laughing. We got in the truck and pulled off.

"I think I'm dying." I glanced in the back seat.

"I'm serious Kruz. You punched me too hard."

"I bet yo ass don't do that shit no more." He waved me off, laid back in the seat and played on the phone. *Dying my ass.*

"Get the fuck out." We were at my house and I regretted having to go in. I hated coming here and couldn't wait until she had my baby.

"If you take a piece of fruit out the bowl, I'ma cut your hands off."

"Eating a piece of fruit ain't stealing." He gave me a dumb smile.

"It is when it ain't yo house."

"You be bugging for nothing. I know not to steal from you." I turned and stared at him.

"Nigga, you know not to steal from everyone but yo punk ass still do it."

"That's because I'm a kid and they let me get away with it." He had a big cheese on his face.

"If the school press charges, guess who ain't getting away with shit?"

"I'm not worried about that. The whole department scared of y'all. Who's really gonna be the one to lock me up?" I opened the door and walked in.

"Don't you worry. I'ma make a call to the station and let them know to keep your trash talking ass down there." I dropped my keys on the table.

"Don't touch shit."

"I'm not dang."

"Matter of fact, let's go." I yoked him up by the collar and made him come upstairs. The whole time Jamaica couldn't stop laughing.

I loved my brother to death but he knows we have way too much money in our family for him to steal. I asked this psychiatrist I met about it and she said he's a kleptomaniac. She also said, some people like stealing because they get a thrill outta it. I've come to realize it's exactly why he does it.

"Tha fuck is going on?" I glanced around my bedroom and saw Zahra hanging clothes up in her old closet. Shoes, purses and everything were in there.

"Looks like she moving back in." My brother said and I tossed his ass on the floor.

"It doesn't make sense for me to have two places Kruz. I gave up my place to stay here." She said that shit as if we spoke about it and I was ok with it.

"Bitch are you crazy?"

"Yea bitch. Are you?" My brother couldn't stand Zahra.

WHAP! My mom smacked the shit outta him.

"Aye! Don't smack him."

"Kruz he shouldn't be cursing."

"And you shouldn't have been helping her move in without my permission."

"The baby needs both parents and..."

"Do you pay bills in this house?" I asked my mother rubbing my temples.

"What?"

"Do you pay bills over here? You know electric, water, gas or something?"

"Well no."

"EXACTLY! So you had no business entertaining her shit." I went in the closet and started removing all her stuff and tossed it down the steps.

"Kruz, what are you doing?"

"Bitch, I said you could stay here until the baby is born, not move the fuck in. If you gave up your spot it's not my problem."

"What's this?" My brother came towards me with a pack of condoms. The box wasn't opened but it didn't matter. It took every bit of strength in me not to strangle her.

"They're old Kruz." My mother stood there speechless.

"Get the fuck out."

"I don't have anywhere to go." She started crying.

"You have room, don't you ma."

"She ain't moving with us." My brother had his arms folded.

"Your mother seems to be her biggest supporter, therefore; it makes sense for her to stay there."

"Don't nobody wanna hear her crying and talking to my other brother about you." I snapped my neck to look at him. Kommon and I may not see eye to eye on a lotta shit but we always got each other's back and trust me, I've had to have his, a lot more than he's had mine. I know damn well he ain't doing no grimy shit. Then again, they've never met.

"What you say?"

"You heard me. When Kommon came over one day, she started telling him all y'all business and one time they left together."

WHAP! My mother smacked him again.

"Boy don't be making up stories."

"I'm not making up shit and don't you hit me again. I'm tired of hiding shit from Kruz. Y'all foul as fuck and I'm telling." Jamaica and I had a look of shock on our face.

"Who you talking to?" I couldn't even chastise his ass for speaking to my mother like that because I was stuck.

"Tell me what you talking about Kash because this don't make sense. They never even met"

"I'll tell you Kruz." She moved in front of me.

"Your brother stopped by and saw me crying. I told him what was going on and he took me out to eat. That's all." She didn't make sense either. How you just up and tell a motherfucker your business and don't know him?

"It don't take five hours to eat." My brother was slowly revealing it all.

"Why were you with him for five hours? You fucking my brother?"

"No Kruz and I wasn't. We ate, I left and came back over. I don't know why Kash is making this more than what it is."

"Fuck you bitch. Bro, she's lying." I didn't know who to believe at this point.

"I may be a thief but I ain't no liar. Kruz, she's grimy. If I were you, I'd follow her or check the phone records."

"Nigga what you know about that?" Jamaica questioned and we both waited for him to answer. Who knew what this little nigga had going on?

"I watch TV." He stood and went downstairs.

"Ma, you knew and didn't tell me?"

"Kruz it was nothing like she said. Kash is overreacting and so are you." I loved how she tried to dismiss the things my brother brought up.

"Well I guess y'all two can stay in cahoots together." I went to the door and turned around.

"If I find out you fucked my brother, I'm gonna kill you, plain and simple." I shrugged my shoulders. I couldn't be mad at the nigga she crept off with unless it was my brother or Jamaica. They know better.

"And ma, I swear if it comes out they did and you knew?"

"Son, they didn't and even if they did and I knew, what are you gonna do to me?" She had a nasty attitude when she said it too. I walked up on her to remind her of who the fuck I really am.

"I probably won't kill you because you are my mother, but I promise to hurt you so bad, you'll never be able to leave the house again. Now fuck with me if you want." She backed away and had a scary look on her face.

"Don't be nervous now ma. You tough and said it's not true, right?" I smiled and walked over to the steps.

"Oh Zahra. If you're not outta here in an hour, I'm gonna come and throw you out. That goes for you too ma." I stormed down the steps and caught Kash looking in the fridge.

"I didn't take anything." He lifted his hands in surrender. I thought about questioning him more but decided against it. He told enough and if some shit is going down with my brother, it'll come out.

"You ok?" I asked Kruz in the restaurant. After talking to him earlier, I dropped Axel off with his father and waited for him to scoop me up. We drove to New York for dinner and I planned on asking if we could stay. I changed my mind because he wasn't in a good mood.

"If someone gave you information while they were angry, would you believe them?"

"Ummmm. I guess it would depend on the news. For instance, did the person who told you have anything to gain from telling you?"

"Nah."

"Ok. Does the person wanna hurt you in any way because words hurt too." He smiled.

"Come here." He sat me on his lap and wrapped his arms around my waist.

"I'm sorry about the conversation you may have overheard between me and my mom. In no way, do I want Zahra or would I place myself in a situation to get hurt again."

"Kruz, we can stop seeing each other until..." His hand went behind my neck as he pulled me in for a kiss.

"Not a chance. You ain't going nowhere." He squeezed my ass and told me to grab my things so we could go.

Once we got to the truck, he drove to fifth avenue and parked. I gave him a crazy look because my ass damn sure didn't have any money to shop on this street. Instead of waiting for me to get out, he opened my door and took my hand in his.

"Are we window shopping because I don't have money for these places?" I pointed at Dior, Louis Vuitton, Prada and all the other name brand stores lined on the street.

"Don't ask questions." We walked in Barney's and my mouth dropped. For one, everything in here is overpriced. And two, the stuff isn't even all that.

"Can I help you Kruz?" The Spanish chick asked and bit down on her lip. It's obvious they know each other and she either slept with him, or wants to.

"Baby, you think she can find me something sexy to model in tonight? I'm always naked so I think it's time to try more stuff." I stood on my tippy toes to kiss him.

200

"Whatever you want sexy. And I'll take you naked over clothes any day. What you got for my girl?" The bitch mouth dropped.

"You know what babe. I'm not feeling this spot. Can we go somewhere else?" I glanced at the tag on a sheer shirt I would possibly wear if I did shop here. It said $450. Whether he had money or not, I'm not even gonna fix my mouth to ask him to get it.

"We got all night." He looked at his watch and grabbed my hand.

"Wait! I can help you here."

"No thanks." I stood in front of her.

"For future reference, when a woman walks in with her man it's inappropriate to blatantly flirt with him. You work on commission, right?"

"Well yes."

"Exactly. And since you're well aware of who he is and how much money he has, say goodbye to his. Smooches." He opened the door for me. See, you don't always have to be ratchet to put a chick in her place. Sometimes the smallest comment will have them in their feelings.

"I like how you put her in her place without bugging. I hate drama. It brings too much unwanted attention."

"As long as no one puts their hands on me, I'll try not to get outta character." He pulled me close and pecked my lips.

"It was hard tho when she bit her lip."

"I am a sexy nigga tho."

"Yea you are. But you're mine so I'm the only one who's supposed to do that." He chuckled and drug me in other stores.

By the time we finished, it was late and neither of us wanted to drive back. He rented a room and the two of us ended up taking a shower together and sat in the jacuzzi for an hour. We didn't actually sit because sex took place but it was still fun and relaxing.

****

"Damnnnnnnnnn bitchhhhh. He brought you mad shit." Kalila shouted when I stepped out Kruz's truck. It was seven in the morning and this heffa was up. We just came back from New York and I still had to spend time with Axel and get ready for work.

"My girl can get whatever she wants even though she complains about the prices. Come here." He put the rest of the bags on the front porch and moved me into his space. It felt good being under him, smelling his cologne and letting him do bad things to my body.

"What you doing after work?"

"Probably going to sleep since someone had me up most of the night."

"Whatever. You loved that shit." He pecked my lips and then put one on my neck.

"Anyway."

"Anyway nothing. Why don't you come over and bring Axel? I have a game system for him to play on."

"Kruz, I don't know. Axel has never met any other man besides his father." He tilted my head with his forefinger.

"I understand Rhythm but I do plan on being around for a while. You may as well let us meet." He glanced down at his phone and said he had to go. We kissed and I watched him pull off.

"Sooooooo?" Kalila had her arms folded.

"So, what?" I grabbed the bags and asked her to help me bring them in.

"Y'all back together again?"

"According to him, we never broke up." I shrugged my shoulders and opened the screen door.

"Let me find out you about to push babies out for that nigga." She locked the door and we crept in the basement. Axel and ma, were still asleep and I wanted to get an hour or so in before he realized I'm home.

"Babies? Not at all."

"Yea ok."

"I'm not you Kalila and strung out." She placed her hand on her heart to show she was offended.

"Bitch, Kenron can get twenty babies outta me if he wants." I started choking at her comment.

"The D must be the shit."

"You have no idea girl." I folded my arms across my chest.

"My best friend isn't in love with her man at all."

"How you figure."

"Bitch, you're only in love with his dick." She and I busted out laughing so hard we had to shhhh each other because it was loud.

"I'm in love with him too. Plus, he's not gonna allow me to ever sleep with anyone else so I may as well love the D."

"They say Jamaican men are crazy." I looked at her to make sure she heard me.

"I know." Her knees were to her chest and she appeared to be nervous. I sat next to her and asked what was wrong.

"He's married."

"Obviously he doesn't love her because he'd be with her instead."

"I know sis but regardless if it's for citizenship or not, do you think if we ever got married he do me the same? I mean, who's to say he won't dip out?"

"Listen Kalila, no woman has ever been able to answer that question. Women do any and everything to please their man, yet; they still go outside the relationship."

"Why is that?"

"Again, if I knew, I'd be rich because my ass would surely be giving out information or advice. I'd charge $500 dollars an hour."

"The day we found out, he brought me home and said if I even think about entertaining another man, he'd slice my throat."

"Well don't sleep with no one else because I don't have time to be tryna sneak him and die with you."

"Him and Kruz would probably stop speaking because he ain't letting no one kill you." She gave me the side eye.

"You think he really likes me?"

"I'm not saying this to make you mad but he did the same for Zahra." I sucked my teeth.

"I don't mean it in a bad way." She rested her hand on my arm and made me look at her.

"What I'm saying is, he started taking care of her when he fell for her. Rhythm, I know Axel hurt you a lot but it's time to let the wall down and let him love you. I don't think he's gonna mess up."

"I hope not because I'm fucking his house up." We got a laugh outta that. I put my pajama pants on and fell asleep. I enjoy every second with Kruz and I pray he doesn't hurt me.

I didn't wanna leave New York with Rhythm but she had to get back to her son and work. I had to handle something with Jamaica because Kandy was up to some grimy shit, just like I knew she would when he made her sign the divorce papers. I hated when a bitch couldn't let go.

In their case its different because they were strictly fuck buddies and only married on paper.

I remember when her dad asked someone to marry her for citizenship. I told my boy not to do it, but he felt because her pops offered up this high position, one of us should do it. He knew my ass wasn't beat and hopped on board. I tried to talk him out of it all the way to the altar but his loyalty is one thing he never swayed away from. I'm not saying he should've but he ain't have no business marrying a bitch when he loved sleeping with other women, daily.

I put the code in to my gate and pulled in to grab a few of my toys. I walked in the door and saw flowers in the living room and kitchen. Thinking Rhythm sent them, I grabbed the card and read it.

Kruz, I'm so sorry about everything and if you take me back, I promise to love you and only you. Is this bitch tryna tell me she's loving another nigga? I called my mother because she's the only one who could've let the people in to deliver these. But then again, I never changed the code so she may have had them done regardless of my throwing her dumb ass out.

"Hello."

"Ma, did you open the door for the delivery people to bring the flowers in?"

"Aren't they pretty son? She spent a lot of money tryna pick the right ones for you. Son, she loves you and I think…" I cut her off in the middle.

"I don't care what you think ma and I'd appreciate if you don't allow the bitch in here. Matter of fact, after today the only way you'll be allowed in here is if I open the gate for you because I'm changing the code."

"Kruz, what on earth has gotten into you? It's the new girl, right?" I made sure the front door was locked and walked up the steps to find heart candy on the bed. Zahra was doing too much.

"Nothing has gotten into me and stop blaming a woman you know nothing about. She isn't making me do anything and if you must know, I didn't meet her until after I found out Zahra cheated."

"Yea, but if she wasn't in the way, you'd be able to forgive Zahra and be a family with my grandbaby."

"Bye ma." I hung up and called my brother Kommon back because he clicked in on the other line.

"What up?" I pressed the button in my closet and picked two of my best guns.

"You busy?"

"Yea. I'm about to head out with Jamaica. What you need?" He stayed quiet in the phone.

"Hello." I had to ask to make sure he was still on it.

"When are you gonna be back because I need to talk to you?"

"Talk now. I got time before I have to meet up with him." I tossed the candy in the trash and sat on my bed.

"What I have to say needs to be said in person." I looked on my nightstand and noticed this stupid bitch left me a card. It's like wherever I looked she left something.

"Bro, just say it. You're starting to piss me off." It wasn't really him I was mad at but he knew I hated for someone to say these needed to talk to you, only to say they'll discuss it later. Why even bring it up?

"I'll hit you up in a few days when you're in a better mood."

"Bet." I hung up and looked around my room. Before I knew it, I was sitting on my computer ordering all new furniture, and even called the rug people. I didn't want any remnants of Zahra here. Yea, the house may be the same but I'm not getting rid of it because I had this built from the ground up before I even met her. This house is humongous and I'll be raising my kids here.

I made sure to contact the people to have the security code on my gate changed, the locksmiths came to change all the locks on my house and I'm having more video cameras installed. If I'm starting over, it had to get it done now. I should've brought my girl here to do it because this shit is aggravating.

****

"You ready to do this?" I asked the ten niggas we've been rocking with since juvie. We were at the house of a up and coming dealer who thought he could rob our spots and come up. It only told me there's a snitch on our team and we're about to find out who it is.

"Yup." Everyone nodded and got in position.

"A'ight. Let's go." I kicked the door opened and there were bitches, kids and niggas everywhere.

"OH SHIT!" One guy shouted and attempted to pull his weapon.

BOOM! I laid his ass out with a hole in his chest from my shotgun.

"OH MY GOD!" A chick tried running and Jamaica took her out. Her brains were on the same wall she slid down.

"Where's Teddy?" I asked as my crew lined everyone up. One of the guys took the kids it the other room. I may be a savage but kids are off limits.

"Please don't kill us." Some other woman cried.

"Why wouldn't we when y'all smoking our shit." I pointed to the package laid out on the table. I know it's ours because all the shit is wrapped in blue foil and that's exactly what's sitting on this table. Little did he know, the spots he robbed had nowhere near as much as the others.

"I only came here to get money from my son's father. Please my baby is over there in the car seat. He needs milk and diapers." We all looked and sure enough there was a baby.

"Why the fuck you got a baby in a trap house?"

"He told me, I could only get money if I came here." She was hysterical crying.

"Yo, get her and the baby the fuck up outta here." She stood and I nodded to my boy Drew.

PHEW! She screamed out when he put a bullet in the top of her leg.

"That's a warning in case you decide to open your fucking mouth. Next time, it'll be in your motherfucking skull. Am I clear?" She shook her head yes and Drew pushed her out the door and placed the baby on the porch.

"Next. Where the fuck he at?"

"YO! Turn the fucking stereo sound down. Y'all got it sounding like real gunshots in here." I smiled at Jamaica when Teddy walked out with the snitch.

"What… are you guys… doing here?" Dallas asked. He was one of the lieutenants who's been with us for a long time.

"Looks like we're getting rid of dead weight."

BOOM! Jamaica chopped his head off with a machete. I told that nigga to bring guns but he said and I quote, *I love feeling body parts detach from people.* And people think I'm the crazy one.

"Where's the rest of our shit?" Teddy had his hands up after he vomited all over the floor.

"Don't kill me. I'm only doing what the guy paid me to do."

"What guy?"

"His name is Geoffrey."

"Geoffrey?"

"Yea. He told me if I robbed you, he'd give me enough money to get me and my family outta the hood."

"Who's your family in here?" I pushed him in the living room where everyone was lined up. He pointed to three dudes, and four females. Two chicks were his sister, and everyone else were his brothers and cousins.

"You can thank me for this later." I pulled my Glock out and made sure each one had a bullet to their head.

PHEW! PHEW! PHEW! PHEW! PHEW! PHEW! PHEW! There were three people left and all of them were crying.

"Jamaica finish this for me." I walked to the back and heard screams. I knew my boy didn't ask no questions and probably killed each one that fast.

"JAMAICA!" I shouted and he came running in. I pointed out the window and his facial expression became even more scary.

"What you wanna do?" I asked regarding Kandy, who jumped out the window and pulled off. It wasn't until she turned around after getting to the car, did I recognize her.

"I got something for her ass." We stepped out the room and checked the place for the remainder of our shit. I grabbed dude and brought him outside. Sadly, his baby mama was lying in the grass barely breathing. I guess the shot in her leg is worse than she thought.

"FUCK! Yo, can I call an ambulance for her?" This nigga didn't even ask about the kid.

"When we're done here." I pushed him against the van.

"I'm not going to kill you Teddy and you know why?"

"Why?"

"I'm gonna let you explain to your family how you're the reason all of them are dead and gone. Then, you can tell your kid, how your baby mom's ain't shit because my boy over there was fucking her." I pointed to my boy Drew. He shrugged his shoulders and picked the kid up.

"Where you going with my baby?" He smirked.

"I've been looking for this bitch for days. Sorry to tell you this bro, but this my son." He placed him in the car and pulled off. I knew once we saw her, he'd want to leave. It's the reason I let her go. The crazy thing is, Drew is the one who shot her. I guess he was mad she came asking another nigga for money when it came to his seed.

"WHAT!!!!!" Teddy was pissed.

"Bitches ain't shit but look here." I could tell he wanted to kill her.

"Tell this Geoffrey dude, when he comes for me and my boy, he needs to come correct and make sure you're protected. Oh, and for future reference don't ever think its ok to approach my girl."

"Your girl?"

"Rhythm." His eyes grew wide. She told me some guy named Teddy approached her at the motel when he rented a room. She mentioned having a man and he became even more persistent. She had to threaten him with the cops, in order for him to leave her alone. Who goes through all that? If the chick says no, then beat it.

"Exactly! Now that we're clear on these few things. Have at 'em guys." I walked away to smoke with Jamaica who was pissed and watched as they damn near beat him to death. I had to make them stop because we needed him to relay the message.

"You good?" I asked my boy when I parked in front of his house.

"Yup. You know it's about to be a war?"

"I'm ready. Just say the word." He gave me a pound and went inside. I pulled off, stopped at Wendy's to grab some food and went home. I smiled when the gate opened because she was standing at the door.

"Why aren't you naked?" I walked up with the food.

"Because I'm hungry and I knew you'd need to clean yourself up first." She pointed to blood on my sneakers.

"Don't act like you know me." She took the bag out my hand. This is the first time she's been in this house but walked around as if she owned it. On the way home, I sent her a text telling her to meet me and gave her the new code to the gate and house.

"I know you a little and I'm not kissing or touching you until you're cleaned up. And don't forget to burn that stuff in the back yard." I had a grin on my face as she walked in the kitchen eating.

"AND DON'T MAKE A MESS ON THE BATHROOM FLOOR. I LOVE THE BLACK MARBLE." I busted out laughing on my way up the steps. She can love it all she wants but it'll be changed soon.

After showering and getting rid of evidence, I heated up my food and joined her on the couch. Fast food doesn't taste the same outta the microwave but when you're hungry, you'll eat anything. We watched a movie and once it was over, I took her upstairs and made love to her all night. It felt good having a woman in my bed, or should I say the guest bed because she wouldn't go in the master bedroom and I didn't blame her.

"How in the hell is he even entertaining the bitch?" I paced in Mrs. Garcia's kitchen.

When Kruz left me speechless two days ago, I didn't take anything from the house. I was too scared he'd return and do damage.

In the four years we were together, he never put his hands on me or tried to hurt me in anyway. But now, it's as if he's an entirely different person. If you didn't know we used to be a couple, you'd have no idea we shared a bed.

I don't understand what he even sees in Rhythm. For one, her name is Rhythm. Who the hell names their child that? Two... she already has a family, therefore; the child won't be his first with her if it ever came down to them reproducing. And third... she doesn't even have a college degree. I mean the bitch works at a damn motel. There's no future with her and I wish he realizes it soon. I'm tired of sleeping alone.

"I'm going to ask you two questions Zahra and I expect the truth." Mrs. Garcia pointed to the chair for me to sit. I stared at her husband walk in. He couldn't stand me either.

"Is that Kruz's baby and did you sleep with anyone close to him?" I swallowed hard and hoped they didn't see me.

"Yes, this is his baby and no I didn't." I wasn't lying about the baby being his. Granted, had the test come back negative I probably would've tried to get someone to change them or ran away. As far as sleeping with someone close to him; shit happens. If he ever found out, both of us would be dead.

"She don't even believe the lies." Kash strolled in playing on his phone.

"Steal one more time nigga and I promise to let Kruz do what he wants to you." Kash lifted his head.

"Ma, why you tell him?"

"I didn't tell. You know I wouldn't put you in harms way." She hugged him.

"That's why he a got damn thief now."

"He's not a thief. He just likes taking things."

"Exactly! A got damn kleptomaniac. Get yo ass ready for school." He hauled ass upstairs.

When they called about him getting arrested I knew Kruz and his father would dig in his ass. Mrs. Garcia is such a sweetheart and never wants to see anyone hurt. It's the reason I came to her. I did think she'd be able to change Kruz mind but he is not budging, which means I have to step my game up.

"What up?" I turned and Kruz brother walked in looking sexy as hell. People often mistake them for twins but they are definitely different in more ways than one.

"Hey son." He gave his father a hug and kissed his mom on the cheek.

"Hey Zahra. How's my brother treating you?" I heard the hint of sarcasm in his voice and the two hickeys on his neck.

"Fine." I pushed my chair out to stand.

"Damn, you're huge."

"Boy, you don't say that to a pregnant woman." His mom popped him in the back of his head like a child.

"Shit, she is huge. You sure it's not two in there?"

"Whatever. I'll see you later."

"Where you going hun. You haven't eaten your breakfast."

"It's ok. I'll stop on the way to the doctors."

"You sure?" I gave her a smile.

"Positive." I walked out the house and to my car. Not only am I excited to see Kruz, I have a plan to win him back.

I noticed the hateful look Kommon had on his face when he stepped on the porch to talk to his dad. Him and his mom weren't close and I'm shocked to even see him here. He's gone so much, I started to believe he was dead or something when Kruz and I first got together. He never came home for holidays and when he did, I think he stayed for a few days and went back out. I didn't meet him until last year. I started my car and pulled off in hopes to win back my boo.

It didn't take me long to get there and I noticed his truck coming in behind me. When he stepped out, I damn near came on myself. His swag is always on point, the diamonds were shining and I've always been in love with his smile. The fact he's smiling on the phone did aggravate me but I'm not gonna let it him know.

"Hey." He nodded and continued his conversation.

"Are you gonna be on the phone for the entire appointment?" He held the door and let it close behind me as he stood outside continuing to talk.

I signed in and took a seat next to a woman and her man. They seemed happy and it's what I wanted with Kruz but he's so stubborn and stuck in his ways. If he just gave me another chance, he'd see I'm where he needs to be. I'm the woman who is having his first child. The woman he loved for four years. You don't just throw it all away for a mistake.

"Zahra Bell." The nurse called and Kruz still hadn't come in. I told her to hold on and went outside to get him.

We both followed her in the back. She had me step on the scale and did my vitals. Afterwards, I sat on the table waiting with my legs swinging. Kruz stood in front of me against the wall with his hands behind him.

"Ok Ms. Bell. This is the last appointment until you deliver. Let's take a look." The doctor had me lie back and turned the machine on. I smiled at my daughter moving around.

"She moves a lot." Kruz said and I placed his hand on my stomach. It's the first time he's touched it since I announced us having a baby. He smiled and a bitch was happier than a kid in the candy store.

"Yea. She's gonna be active. Do you want one more picture?" He told her yes and printed one out.

"Remember sex can help during the delivery process." Kruz looked up from his phone when she said it.

"Bitch, you better not fuck that nigga with my daughter in there."

"KRUZ!"

"What? We not together and I don't know what the fuck you out there doing."

"Sex may not be an option but walking helps too." The doctor said goodbye and moved swiftly out the room. I pulled my leggings over waist and stepped off the stool.

"That wasn't necessary Kruz."

"Says who, you?" He opened the door and I closed it back.

"We may not be together but it doesn't change the fact I still love you. I'm having your daughter and you treat me like the dirt on your shoe." I put my hand on the side of his face and took a chance. When our lips met and he didn't stop me, I rushed to get his jeans down. He never wore a belt and let them sag so it was easy.

"Oh shit." I wrapped my mouth around his dick and sucked like my life depended on it. I stared up and noticed him looking down at me. I couldn't read his demeanor but he definitely enjoyed it.

He pushed me off, backed up and released all over my face. I didn't know if I should feel disrespected or what. He walked over to the sink, grabbed some paper towels, wet them with water and soap and cleaned himself up. I struggled to stand and grabbed some tissue out the box.

"I fucked up Zahra and allowed my old feelings to get in the way but make no mistake.-" I was still wiping his cum off my face.

"I'm with someone else and I messed up letting you kiss and go down on me." I sucked my teeth because he claimed the bitch.

"But what's more mind boggling, is the fact you gave me head after four years and knew exactly what to do." I'm not even sure why I did it for him and not Kruz.

"Kruz." He put his hand up to finish speaking.

"You played with my balls, jerked me good, spit and everything." The guy I cheated with showed me how to do it. I was gonna do him but he broke up with me.

"All you did was show me you been sucking that nigga dick." I let the tears fall from my eyes because he's right. There was so much hurt in his voice and on his face I'm not sure we'll recover after this.

"Don't call me until you deliver." He opened the door and a nurse had her hand up to knock.

"KRUZZZZZ!" I screamed and fell against the wall crying. How could I be stupid to do it? I should've waited and pretended to let him show me.

I grabbed my stuff and stormed out the doctors off. Someone's gonna feel my wrath, starting with the bitch at my mother's house.

****

It's been six days, five hours and twenty-seven minutes since the situation at the hospital and all I've done is sit in this stupid ass hotel room. I thought he'd call and check on me but nope. His mother said, he went to Mexico the day after we saw the doctor. I asked if he took the bitch and she wasn't sure. He told her, he'd see her once he came back.

Now I'm on the way to my mother's house in hopes to find out something. I haven't been here in a while either because I was trying to keep my distance from my shady ass sister, and depressing mother. I still can't believe the two of them are ok with Rhythm sleeping with my man. We're about to have a child together and I'm not about to deal with Kruz neglecting her or even tryna have the bitch help raise her.

I parked in front of my mothers and not one car sat in the driveway. I waddled to the door, stuck my key in and walked straight inside. I was amazed by how much different it

228

looked. The downstairs was already nice but the upstairs is complete and a bitch is hating.

There used to be three bedrooms but they added two. The bathroom was huge and so were each of the bedrooms. The furniture was beautiful and even Axel's room had a nice look. Minecraft posters, a video game, TV on the wall and his closet's full of clothes. I can't assume Kruz did anything because truth be told, Axel's father and his family take good care of him.

Something told me to go in the connecting room and to say a bitch is pissed would be an understatement. I wasn't sure it was her room until I saw unopened mail on the dresser.

The closet was full of expensive ass bags. I mean Gucci, Fendi and tons of other stuff. There were clothes with price tags on them and shoes I know the bitch can't pronounce. She has to be fucking him because her baby daddy may be good to her son but he damn sure ain't to her. He cheated, gave her a disease and lives with his new girlfriend.

I was so mad, I started ripping shit off the hangers and tossing them out the window. All the bags, shoes and even the expensive looking comforter graced the back yard. I didn't care who found out I did it. My anger got the best of me so bad, I ran downstairs, got the biggest knife and cut up her mattresses, pillows, sheets, and even the rug. Rhythm is not about to benefit off my child's father.

After I calmed down, I put the knife in the sink and walked out feeling ten times better mentally. Physically, I was fucked up because the pain in my stomach became unbearable. I didn't know if these were contractions but whatever they are, made me hold on the railing and scream out.

A few people outside ran over asking me if I was ok. Once the inside of my pants became wet, someone called 911. Not even five minutes later the EMT's pulled up at the same time my sister and Jamaica did. *What are they doing together if they're not fucking?*

"Thanks Mr. Kruz, I had a good time in Mexico." Rhythm's son said when we got off the plane.

The day I fucked up at the doctor's office with Zahra, I picked up Rhythm and her son and went to Mexico. I needed a vacation and since we've become so close I didn't wanna go without her.

At first, she told me no and I had done enough for her with the shopping sprees. But once I told her the tickets were already paid for, she broke and came. The funny thing is, I owned a jet and we left from a private airport. I brought Kash with us so her son wouldn't he bored. Her and my brother hit it off good too. He did ask if she or Kalila had any little sisters. *Nasty motherfucker.*

I had to tell Kash he better not teach him how to steal and if he did while we were out there, I was gonna feed him to the sharks. Jamaica and Kalila came to chill on the third day and we had a ball.

During our time there, we toured a bunch of different spots, took Axel and Kash to different water parks and of course shopping. Rhythm didn't have a lot of money but she did pay for dinner every night and I appreciated it. The little things meant a lot more to a nigga than trying to impress me with other stuff.

The last night in Mexico, Rhythm and I had the freakiest sex ever. Nothing is off limits as it is, but we were outside on the beach doing anything to one another. When we finished, she confessed falling in love with me. She also admitted, it's probably because she's been single for so long it wasn't hard. I told her in these last six months, I felt the same because I did.

Rhythm is like a breath of fresh air for me. She's a great mother to her son and her loyalty to Kalila and her mom is commendable, which is why Jamaica and I furnished the entire upstairs of their newly renovated house. Well, we gave them the money because I damn sure don't have time to shop.

"Anytime, lil man." All four of us got in the truck and I drove to drop Kash off first. I offered for her to come in and she gave me the finger.

"Ma, can you drop me off at the hospital and take the truck?" I hopped in and sped off. My father said, my mother just left because Zahra was about to deliver. I was both excited and disappointed because I hated who my child's mother is gonna be.

"Yea, is everything ok?"

"Zahra's in labor."

"Really! Are you excited?" She had a smile on her face. I thought she'd be upset but I guess being on your grown woman shit, won't allow it.

"Yes and no." I pulled off in route to the hospital.

"Yes, because she's my daughter and no, due to who mother is."

"Well, you picked her." We both laughed.

I parked in front of the hospital, and waited for her to get in the driver's seat. We kissed, I watched her pull off and ran in to ask where the labor and delivery floor is. Once she told me, I couldn't get there fast enough.

"Is she here yet?" I asked my mother who was coming out the room.

"Not yet. They're prepping her and the doctor said she isn't fully dilated yet."

"Oh." I went over to the chairs and sat down.

"You're not going in?"

"For what?"

"To see your daughter being born." I leaned back in the chair and stared at her. How could a woman support another doing dumb shit is beyond me?

"Honestly, I'm not sure if the kid is mine." We may have taken the test and they confirmed it, however; after Zahra sucked my dick, I was convinced she had been with that nigga for much longer than she said. There's no way in hell she gave him head once and did it with no problem. She's a nurse too, which means she could've had the results changed.

"Kruz why are you treating her like this? Four years is a long time to flush the relationship down the drain." I hopped up and got in her face. My phone started vibrating but whoever it is had to wait. I needed to say this shit and make sure she heard me.

"I didn't make shit go down the drain. She did when she started spending time with someone else. You seem to forget that I'm the one you birthed and not her."

"Son. I'm..."

"I'm over the bullshit with you and her. We aren't ever getting back together and when you see me with Rhythm, you better not disrespect or challenge her."

"She's your woman now?"

"Yup and you or Zahra ain't changing it." I snatched the phone off my hip and answered, still looking at her.

"Hello." Rhythm was distraught and I could barely understand her.

"Babe, I don't mean to call at a time like this but she fucked up everything. My entire room is destroyed and..."

"Hold on. Who did what?" I told her to calm down and speak slow.

"I came home after dropping you off and went to give Axel a bath. Kruz, everything you brought is thrown out in the backyard. She either took a knife or scissors to my bed, sheets and rug. I know it's Zahra because her car is parked in front of the house and it wasn't a break in."

"I'ma handle it."

"Kruz, my son is asking who would do this to my room. I can't tell him she did it because he loves her."

"Babe, I got you. Relax and I'll be there after she delivers." I hung up and put the phone on my hip.

"You're going to her while Zahra's in labor?" I stopped and turned around.

"I'd quit while I was ahead or you're gonna regret it." She saw my face and put her hands up in surrender.

I stormed in the room, yanked this dumb bitch up by the hair and made her look at me. I could hear the machine beeping fast and her holding her stomach and gave zero fucks. What she did is unacceptable and she's about to hear my mouth.

"What you did was childish as fuck and I'm gonna make sure you're dealt with after having this baby."

"Kruz please stop." Her hands were tryna pry mine off.

"Shut the fuck up bitch. You're lucky this is all I'm doing." I slammed her head in the pillow and turned to see her mother walking in.

WHAP! She smacked fire from Zahra.

"How dare you come in my house and destroy her room like that?" I stared down at the pictures Rhythm sent and got mad all over again.

"Ma, she don't deserve him."

"Oh, and a woman who's been opening her legs to God knows who during a relationship does?" Zahra put her head down.

"I raised you better than this and I pray my granddaughter doesn't grow up doing the same." She cursed Zahra out after each contraction and I didn't feel bad. My mother stood there watching and I dared her to say a word.

After ten hours of being in labor, my daughter finally graced us with her presence. She weighed seven pounds and 6 ounces. My mom said she looks just like me but she would say that being she's team Zahra. I ended up calling my pops up and asked him to come get her. The slick comments about us being a couple again were getting on my damn nerves.

****

The next day, the picture people came and so did Kalila and Jamaica. My mom strolled in with my father and brother Kash. Most of the conversations were with me because no one could stand Zahra but my mom and for good reason.

I handed Sasha back to her mother and went to use the bathroom. When I came out Rhythm and Axel were standing at the door. She said he wanted to see his auntie's baby. It's sad that Zahra can't stand his mother because of jealousy and he loved her to death. I pulled her in for a kiss and whispered how much I missed her.

"TiTi Zahra." She looked up and smiled but rolled her eyes when I sat Rhythm on my lap.

"Hey baby. How are you?"

"I'm fine but somebody messed up mommy's room. They cut up everything. Do you know who did it because I saw your car at the house? Did you see the person?" He bombarded her with questions.

238

"I did it." All of us got quiet. I moved Rhythm off my lap because shit is about to get crazy. Zahra's mom told her to shut the fuck up in a nice way but as usual, her ass didn't listen.

"Why would you do that to mommy?" He was confused as hell.

"Because I hate your mother and if I could kill her, I would."

"OH MY GOD!" My mom shouted. Rhythm tried to jump on the bed but my dad caught her just in time.

"GET MY SON OUTTA HERE!" She screamed and my mother actually took him out. One thing my mom doesn't play is, saying or doing ignorant shit around kids.

"You's a stupid bitch. Why the fuck would you say some dumb shit like that to a kid?"

"Because I do hate her. I hate everything about her." I stared at Rhythm who was tryna calm down.

"Why the fuck did you have to come in our life? Bitch, Kalila is my sister and she's my mother."

"Get off me. I don't care if she just had a baby. I'm about to beat her ass."

"You ain't doing shit." Zahra picked my baby up. She knew like I did, Rhythm wouldn't touch her.

"I'm fine Mr. Garcia. Put me down." He did and she fixed her clothes.

"You acting like you're better than me. Like your pussy good enough for him not to stray. Well guess what?" I knew right then shit was about to be fucked up.

"Last week at the doctors."

"Shut yo ass up Zahra."

"Nah. Fuck you and her."

"Last week we kissed in the doctor's office and I sucked him off." Rhythm looked at me and so did everyone else. I've never been a cheater and they all knew how I felt about Rhythm, well except my mother because she was in denial. I'm sure they're wondering why, the same way I am.

"That's right bitch. Then he took your dumb ass to Mexico to try and cover up his guilt. Bitch, I ain't going nowhere. We got years in." The tears rolling down Rhythm's

240

face fucked me up. I should've never kept this from her knowing the type of person Zahra is. The sad part is she just told me in Mexico how much in love with me, she was.

"Ok then." She walked up on me.

"Here's the keys to your truck, your house in Sayreville and the condo downtown." She dug in her purse to get them.

"Sayreville? Condo?" Zahra questioned and I kept my eyes on Rhythm.

"You should've known about these places since you have time in but let me clear Zahra." She moved closer but I stood in between.

"I'm not gonna cause a scene because it's no need." She said but I wasn't taking a chance. Rhythm was that mad.

"Years in with a nigga don't mean shit as you can tell."

"Whatever."

"Now its whatever because you see I got the keys to his shit but here." She passed them to her and I snatched them right outta Zahra's hand. I wish the fuck I would let her have them.

"You were right about one thing and that's, that you two belong together." She wiped her face, grabbed her purse and walked out with Kalila behind. I tried to go after her but my father told me to give her space. I stared at this bitch and had she not been holding Sasha I probably would've strangled her. My father had to hold me back.

"What's up?" My brother Kommon strolled in smiling.

"What up?" He gave me a hug and something was off. I knew when shit wasn't right with him and he knew too because his smile turned into a slight frown.

"You here to see your niece?"

"My niece?" He questioned.

"Yea. This dumb bitch just had my daughter."

"Your daughter? Nah bro. I'm here to see my daughter."

"Nigga, I ain't no you had a kid. Ma, did you know?" I asked when she stepped in.

"Kommon, you never told me about any kids." Confusion was written on everyone's face except his and Zahra's. Then I remembered what Kash said.

242

"Zahra said she told you it was a chance the baby may not be yours."

"What the fuck you just say?"

"I told you Kruz but nobody wanted to listen to me." Kash said sitting in the chair.

"You heard me. Now where's the nurse so we can get a test done. I'm either the father or the uncle." All I saw was red.

Rhythm

I walked out the room with Kalila holding my hand, hurt, humiliated and embarrassed. I definitely knew about the doctor's appointment but the rest remained a secret until she blasted it. Who knew she hated me so much she'd blurt it out to my child. My poor baby covered his ears and started crying. He was devastated and everyone in the room knew it.

"Come on sweetie." I lifted him up out of Kruz's mom arms. She had the nerve to ask if he's gonna be ok, as if she cares.

"You don't have to worry about this one here."

"Rhythm. I'm..."

"You're what? Sorry." I looked her up and down. This woman was pathetic and I didn't care to hear any fake ass apologies.

"You're not sorry one bit. This is what you wanted right? You did any and everything possible to try and keep them together. Made her weasel back in the house, buy things for the baby and go to doctors' appointments." The insurance guy who left his card at the motel walked past us and went to the bitch's room. How did they know each other?

"Let's go sis." Kalila took my hand in hers.

"I understand why you felt he should go to the doctors but what you should've done is taken the time out to be his mother, and not hers." She sucked her teeth and we walked off. I turned and saw her going in Zahra's room.

"Effff him sis." I laughed at Kalila because I know she wanted to say more and didn't. We really tried our hardest not to curse in front of him.

I placed Axel in the back of the Uber called and put his seatbelt on. Neither of us had a car here and this was our only option unless I got the keys back from Zahra and drove his truck.

I leaned my head on the window and closed my eyes. Why in the hell did I end up falling in love with a man who's clearly not over his ex?

The Uber stopped in front of the house and Kalila helped me pack some things for me and my son. There're a few vacancies at the motel and I asked our boss if I could occupy one. I told him someone broke in my house and I'm scared to stay there. He's cool and pretty much lets me do whatever since I've been working here right outta high school.

I never got the chance to experience college because of my son. I don't regret him one bit, however; I do think about if I'd have a better job had I went to school. Maybe not because Kalila graduated and she still can't get a good paying job no matter how many applications she put out.

"Hey, can I drop Axel off until tomorrow?" I asked his father's mom. She loved my son and hated when I picked him up.

"Yes girl. You don't ever have to ask." I hung up and packed him some games too. The three of us left in my car, I dropped him off at his grandmothers and headed to the motel with my best friend next to me.

I went in the office, spoke to the chick working and grabbed a key to the room next door to the office. The boss stayed here sometimes if he had to work and no one could cover, which is rarely. The room is basically a one-bedroom apartment.

It's actually nice in here, minus the ugly ass picture he has hanging in the living room. It's a big black tiger with blue eyes he said, he had to have. I asked why doesn't he put it in his own house? He said, it was expensive and his wife would kill him if she knew he brought it.

The kitchen is small but big enough for a square table and two chairs. The bathroom is a decent size and the bedroom has a nice set in here, thanks to me. He offered me to stay here a few years ago but I didn't wanna move. I furnished the place and even put an exercise bike in to work out. It's gonna do for now.

I wasn't worried about Ms. Bell losing the house anymore because it's paid off and so is the loan. I'm still waiting to hear back about the person putting all those things in my name. Thankfully, the guy put in for fraud so it's not on my credit report.

I never called the insurance guy and I'm glad I didn't if he's affiliated with Kruz. Not saying he'd do me dirty but I don't need him telling my business.

"You ok Rhythm?" Kalila was sitting on the couch texting when I stepped out the shower.

"Yea. I knew he was too good to be true."

"Rhythm, I'm not taking his side but do you think Zahra did it on purpose?"

"What you mean?" I put lotion in my hands and then my legs.

"She had him going to those appointments probably tryna get them alone. He probably had a moment and didn't mean to mess up."

"Really?"

"I'm just saying. He really does love you and I don't think you should take him back if you don't want too. However; I do believe my sister planned all of this, down to exposing him in front of you."

"Oh. I don't doubt that at all. I just wanna know why did he allow her to even get that far?"

"The only person who can answer that is him." She stood and went to the window.

"Yup and I don't wanna hear the excuses so its best we part ways. Kalila, are you listening?" I asked because she was occupied at the window.

"Bitch, it's those niggas again and they leaving."

"What niggas?" I walked over to where she was and peeked out.

"The ones hiding shit in the room."

"Ok and..." I moved when the van pulled off.

"And they left. Let's go see what they hiding."

"Girl, are you crazy?"

"Yup and so are you? Put your slippers on." I blew my breath, grabbed the key to my room and followed her to the front desk. I told the chick she could take a half hour break because we'll be here. It's the only way we could grab their key and go in the room. It would give us time to go in and come back.

"You ready?" Kalila grabbed my hand and we walked down passed all the doors. We made it to the room, looked around and didn't see any cars coming.

"Hurry up bitch before we get caught." She barked because it was taking time to get in.

"I think they did something to the lock." I kept jiggling the key until the door finally opened. Both of us rushed in and closed the door.

"Shit! Where's the light?" I moved my hands around on the wall and felt a body.

"Really Kalila. Move so I can turn it on."

"Heffa, I'm over here." Her voice came from a different direction and at that very moment, I knew we fucked up coming in here.

"If you're over there, then who is..."

"Didn't we tell you nosy bitches to stay out this room?" His voice sent chills down my spine and not good ones.

CLICK! I felt the cold gun on my temple.

"Rhythm you have to see this shit in the bathroom." Dude turned the lights on and Kalila froze.

"Lord please forgive me for my sins and watch over my son." I said out loud and asked myself, why in the hell did I listen to this crazy ass girl?

K: *Babe, you need to get to the hospital.*

Me: *What's wrong? You ok?*

K: *Yea. Zahra blasted Kruz in front of Rhythm about them sleeping together and it's a mess.*

Me: *A'ight. I'll be there shortly.*

I dropped my girl off earlier to visit her sister and newborn niece. I planned on going in too because it's my boys' baby but other things had to be taken care of. Such as me walking into this restaurant to meet up with Kandy. I'm not going to re kindle no flame or have sex. I'm good with my girl and I'm not tryna lose her again.

"What's the deal? You tryna send yo new nigga after me?" I blurted out the second we made eye contact. She had a seat in the back of the place. It wasn't packed and the few people there seemed to be in their own world.

"Have a seat Jamaica."

"I'm good standing."

"Suit yourself." She picked her fork up and continued eating as if my presence meant nothing. I knocked everything

252

off the table, snatched her up by the shirt and pushed her against the wall.

"You know I'm not into games."

"Jamaica please let me go." She attempted to pry my hands off but it was no use because my grip was tight.

"Tell me what you got planned with him."

"How can I when you have me against the wall?" I released my grip and slammed her hard in the chair.

"Are you ok?" Some woman walked over being nosy.

"Mind your business." She backed away.

"Jamaica, I think you should rethink the divorce. I mean you have much to lose." I gave her a crazy look.

"I ain't got shit to lose. You on the other hand are playing a dangerous game."

"Kalila Bell isn't worth losing?" I put my gun under her chin and my knee in her stomach. I don't give a fuck about her claiming to be being pregnant. It ain't my motherfucking kid.

"What did you do?" She smiled and put her hand on top of mine.

"You think I'm playing?"

POW!

"OH MY GOD!" She screamed. I shot her foot and put the gun back under her chin. People were running out the place.

"Let's try this again.

"I didn't do it. He did."

"Speak."

"The guy I'm messing with said I couldn't divorce you because my name attached to yours, held a lot of weight."

"You're not making any sense."

"All I know is he's aware of you putting a gun under my chin."

"Because you told him, not that I care. What does that have to do with anything?"

"He found out about the woman you've been with and at this very moment sent someone to find her." I pushed myself off her and backed away.

"What the fuck you mean?" She tried to nurse her foot that was bleeding profusely but I smacked her hand away.

"One of the guys you have working for you is his cousin and he's looking for her." I smacked the fuck outta her dumb ass.

"This is all your fault."

"Jamaica, I…"

"Bitch don't say a fucking word and you need to pray nothing happens to my girl because if it does, I promise I'll be back for you." I walked out the restaurant and noticed a black truck sitting on the opposite side of the street. Never being the one to show fear, I walked over, tapped on the glass and waited for the window to come down. When it did, I was shocked as hell.

"Tha fuck you doing here? It's a long way from home." I said to my father. He moved back to Jamaica a few years ago because my mom no longer wanted to be here. Unfortunately, she passed away when someone robbed the bank she was in.

"I'm here to kill my ex best friend's daughter."

"What? Why is that?" I was confused as shit, yet; still needed to find my girl. My phone went off and I ignored it for the moment.

"Kandy's mother killed your mom, so it's only right I take someone from them" He blew the smoke out his cigar.

"Pops, you know moms died in a random act of violence." He smirked and handed me an envelope.

"When you live in the world we live in, they're never random acts."

"What's this?"

"Proof that she's involved in your moms killing. Read it over and come see me at the Marriott when you finish doing whatever you're about to do." The window went up and his truck pulled off. I looked down at my phone because it kept going off. There were missed calls from Kruz's father and a text from Kalila. I hauled ass to my car.

"What the fuck is that?" I noticed a van in front of me with a body hanging out. The person pointed something in my direction.

SWISH! I heard and watched as a MANPAD flew in my direction. It's a small anti-aircraft missile used to target helicopters and other small things. Everything happened so fast, I had no other choice but to face the inevitable.

BOOM!!!!!

TO BE CONTINUED...

Made in United States
North Haven, CT
19 December 2021

13277345R00143